T0158918

STREET CRED

STREET CRED

C.W. SPOONER

STREET CRED

iUniverse books may be ordered through booksellers or by contacting:

iUniverse
1663 Liberty Drive
Bloomington, IN 47403
www.iuniverse.com
1-800-Authors (1-800-288-4677)

ISBN: 978-1-5320-5789-2 (sc)
ISBN: 978-1-5320-5788-5 (e)

Library of Congress Control Number: 2018910850

Print information available on the last page.

iUniverse rev. date: 09/11/2018

For three of Steffan Manor's finest:
Roger Ashlock, who shared the experience;
Jerry Warren, for that classic '46 Ford convertible;
and Bruce Bigelow, who knows why—or should.

Also by C.W. Spooner:

'68—A Novel
Children of Vallejo
Yeah, What Else?
Like a Flower in the Field

PRELUDE

The North Bay city of Vallejo, California, was awake before first light on this June day in 1970. Women toiled in their kitchens, eggs and bacon frying, biscuits baking, and rich black coffee steaming in heavy mugs. Their men buttoned blue work shirts, buckled worn leather belts, and laced up their boots. Lunch pails sat on countertops, packed by loving hands. A hearty breakfast, a kiss goodbye, and out the door they went.

Most of the men heading off to work were bound for Mare Island Naval Shipyard—The Yard for short. Others would find their way to the Benicia Arsenal, or Sperry Mills, or C&H Sugar over in Crockett. On the way, they would pass the night shift crews, heading home for a well-earned rest.

Vallejo was proud of its Navy heritage. From its founding in 1854, The Yard became the chief maintenance depot for the Pacific Fleet, builder of a long line of warships, and later the West Coast base of nuclear submarine construction. Mare Island had launched seventeen nuclear subs, beginning with the USS *Sargo* in 1957. Seven of that number were what the sailors called boomers, armed with nuclear-tipped Polaris missiles. These proud ships carried the names of American icons: *Theodore Roosevelt, Andrew Jackson, Woodrow Wilson, Daniel Boone, Stonewall Jackson, Kamehameha,* and *Mariano G. Vallejo* himself.

Nineteen seventy was a busy time in Vallejo. The war in Vietnam was at its peak and war meant jobs for Mare Island. Civilian employment on the shipyard hovered around twelve thousand with no drop-off in sight. In addition, the city had committed to urban redevelopment, locking in federal funds for a massive project to rebuild the blighted downtown district known as Lower Georgia.

Georgia Street, the main street of town, ended at the waterfront. The final two blocks of Georgia and several surrounding streets had evolved into a city within a city, packed with bars, gambling dens, whorehouses, and more blazing neon than anywhere in the country, Las Vegas excepted. A popular business model went as follows: a bar as one came in off the street, gambling in the back room, prostitution upstairs. Lower Georgia was notorious throughout the Pacific Fleet as a place for young sailors to raise hell.

And raise hell they did!

Shipyard commanders, likely reaching back to David G. Farragut, demanded a cleanup of the district. City fathers, on the other hand, wanted the sailors coming ashore on liberty to confine their activities to Lower Georgia and stay out of the decent neighborhoods. Under threat and pressure from the Navy, periodic efforts were launched to crack down on vice. Those efforts were short-lived.

By June 1970, all of that had changed. Lower Georgia was gone, razed, flattened. One hundred twenty-five acres stood ready for redevelopment. Of course, mistakes had been made along the way. Historic buildings that should have been preserved were demolished along with the honky-tonks and cathouses, including the YMCA, the Carnegie Library, and the Women's Club designed by famed architect Julia Morgan. Even the York Street hill, where the state capitol building once stood, had been bulldozed and leveled, the earth used as landfill in the marshlands along the waterfront.

Vallejoans would look back on this time as a tipping point. In May, just a month earlier, The Yard had celebrated the launch of the USS *Drum*, a fast-attack sub of the Sturgeon class. It would be the last of the nuclear ships built at Mare Island, and the long, slow decline toward base closure would begin, culminating in April 1996.

None of that was known to the workers heading out that morning. They couldn't know the *Drum* would be the last, or that Vallejo would decline in tandem with the shipyard. It was just another workday in a blue-collar, lunch-pail town.

There was one small exception.

1

icholas Shane Jr. sat behind the wheel of his 1946 Ford convertible coupe, turned the key, and engaged the starter. He listened to the rumble of the flathead V-8 and turned on the windshield wipers to clear away morning dew. He shifted into first gear, let out the clutch, and pulled away from the curb. Nick had no idea what lay ahead, but he was ready for the adventure.

At the end of the block, he made a left onto Georgia Street, accelerating into the light traffic along the broad, tree-lined boulevard. He loved the sound of the old Ford, enhanced by the dual pipes and glass-pack mufflers he and his dad had installed. They'd purchased the vehicle for two hundred dollars from a neighbor and then poured hours into the classic coupe, tuning the engine, replacing hoses and brake linings, cleaning and polishing the dark gray exterior. All it needed now was a new convertible top. That was where he and his dad had left it, just before the heart attack. Nicholas Shane Sr. was gone at sixty-two.

Nick crossed the I-80 overpass, heading west, his dad's beat-up lunch pail resting on the seat beside him. Today was different from all other workdays. Today, June 15, 1970, Nick would go to work for the Vallejo Street Department.

Nick was suddenly aware of his boots: the oiled leather and white crepe soles unblemished, pristine, fresh out of the box labeled Red Wing Shoes. Geez, why hadn't he thought to stomp around a field somewhere just to get 'em dirty? He looked around the corporation yard where a group of thirty men gathered, talking, laughing, smoking, and waiting for the day's assignments. Were they gesturing toward him and snickering, or was he imagining? It was conspicuous enough to be twenty years old, starting work with a group of men who looked to be in their fifties, if not older. He'd made it worse by showing up in these damn boots.

Gus Cordeiro, superintendent of the Street Department, strode into the center of the group and took charge. Gus was short and round, his olive complexion reflecting his Portuguese heritage. He looked younger that his fifty years, even though his hairline was in serious retreat. His men knew him as an affable, empathetic boss, quick with a laugh and a barbed comment, but a man you did not cross when he took a stand.

"All right, listen up." Gus waited for one noisy group to finish their conversation. "Hey! Are you guys through? Can I get your attention over here?" It grew quiet. "Sorry to interrupt, ladies." He grinned at the offenders. "Okay, we have a new man with us, his first day on the job. Say hello to Nick Shane. Nick, step up and take a bow."

Nick took a step forward in his new boots and raised his hand. He smiled and nodded as voices around the yard chimed in with variations of, "Hi, Nick … Welcome aboard … Good luck, kid; you're gonna need it …"

Gus called for order and began the assignments for the day. A crew would continue paving a block of Tennessee Street. Two teams would work sidewalk repair out in Steffan Manor. A group would be on loan to the Parks Department for tree-pruning duty. And so it went. Nick would ride with a guy named Wally, patching potholes, whatever that meant. The men began to disburse, heading toward the lot where trucks and heavy equipment were parked.

Gus motioned to Nick. "Come on. I'll get you set up."

At one side of the yard stood a long, low shed, the metal doors rolled up. The building housed lockers, assorted small tools and supplies. Gus directed Nick to choose a locker. He handed Nick a new flat-headed shovel, the only tool he would need.

"Put your stuff in the locker—jacket, rain gear, whatever. Stow your shovel in there at night. It's your space. Did you bring gloves? Good. Come and meet your partner."

Nick followed Gus toward two men standing a few lockers away, one wearing a neatly pressed work shirt and spotless khakis, the other a battered jacket, faded baseball cap, and soiled denim pants.

Gus made the introductions. "Wally Grover, this is Nick Shane." The neatly dressed man smiled and extended his hand. Nick shook it firmly. Gus turned toward the other man. "Mike Bouchka, meet Nick Shane."

Mike kept his right hand in the front pocket of his pants. He reached out to Nick with his left hand and Nick accepted the awkward gesture. Mike looked to be in his sixties, and his complexion was an odd shade of gray. He didn't speak.

Gus continued. "Wally, Nick is going to ride with you for a few days. Teach him everything he needs to know about potholes." Gus and Wally laughed.

Mike's downcast gaze found Nick's shoes. "Nice boots, kid." The old man's voice sounded like a growl. He broke into a lopsided smile while Nick's cheeks turned red.

Wally patted Mike on the shoulder and turned toward Nick. "Welcome to the crew, Nick. Got your shovel? Okay, come on and we'll get started." He led Nick toward the back of the yard, leaving Mike with Gus. "We'll take number fifty-one over here." He gestured toward a large International Harvester dump truck, painted hunter green and bearing the City of Vallejo decal. "Everything you need to know about potholes? Ha! That'll take about five minutes. You can put your shovel on the side of the bed there. Give me a hand with the tailgate."

Wally threw the lever that released the tailgate and Nick helped lower it to a horizontal position. Wally walked over to a battered old front-loader and started the engine. The machine came to life and he backed it away from its stall and drove a short distance to a large bin piled high with asphalt. The scoop lowered and Wally drove forward to pick up a couple of yards of the black material. Nick admired the man's skill as he maneuvered into position, raised the scoop, and dropped the load into the bed of the truck. A minute later the old loader was back in its resting place. Nick and Wally secured the tailgate and then climbed into the cab of the truck.

"Okay, Nick, here's the drill." Wally turned and smiled in Nick's direction. "We just drive around looking for potholes—you know, places where the pavement has broken up and left a hole. When we find one, we throw some asphalt in there, tamp it down, maybe drive over it. And that's it. Easy money, am I right?"

"Is this your usual job?" Nick turned toward his partner. Neat, well-groomed, about five ten, weighing a buck seventy-five, Wally stood out from the rest of the crew.

"No, not always. I'm a certified heavy equipment operator. When we've got a major paving job, I drive the Caterpillar grader.

And the dozer, if we need it. But we're not doing major projects every day."

"Where'd you learn heavy equipment?"

"In the Navy. I was a Seabee—construction battalion—during the war." Wally exited the corporation yard and turned left onto Amador Street. "Gus wants us to work the downtown area today. We'll get an early start before the stores open." He turned right onto Georgia Street and headed west. "Old Mike usually rides with me. I think Gus has something else for him the next few days."

"Mike seems ... quiet." Nick paused, hoping Wally would take the cue. "How long has he been on the job?"

"Well, that's a long story." Wally downshifted as they started up the steep Georgia Street hill. "But then, we've got all day."

2

They cruised the several blocks of the downtown shopping district, halting now and then to patch holes in the pavement. Wally would stop just beyond the offending fissure, raise the bed of the truck about forty-five degrees, and they'd jump out and grab their shovels. When the hole was filled and tamped down, Wally would lower the bed and they'd move on. In between stops, he gave Nick a rundown of the Mike Bouchka story.

"Mike hired in right after the war. This is '70, so it's been about twenty-five years. He's retired Navy, like a lot of our guys. Anyway, about six months ago he had a stroke. His right arm is weak, and his balance is a little off." Wally turned right and headed east on Virginia Street. "You notice he doesn't say much, and the right side of his face sags a little. He talks, but it's an effort. The guys joke around with him and get him to laugh, and you'll hear him say, 'You rotten SOB!' when they play a prank on him. But that's about it."

"But he's still out here, working?"

"Well, he doesn't do much anymore. But was he a workhorse before the stroke. Really set the bar for all of us." Wally paused and glanced at Nick. "See, the thing is, he's about a year away from full retirement. We're gonna see to it that he gets there. With a city pension and his Navy benefits, he and his wife will be okay."

"And Gus is okay with this?"

"Oh, yeah. Gus … well, Gus is all heart. Know what I mean? It was probably his idea."

Wally stopped for a pothole and raised the truck bed. Nick climbed down from the cab and grabbed his shovel, thinking about his friend and mentor, Gustavo "Gus" Cordeiro. What a guy! Nick had Gus to thank for this job, the chance to bank some much-needed cash toward his college plans.

Back in the cab, Wally glanced at his watch. "How 'bout a cup a coffee, Nick? It's about 9:30. Time for a break."

"Sounds good. Is there a place around here?"

"Oh, yeah. That's one thing you'll learn on this job. Before long you'll know every coffee shop in town with an alley in the back where you can hide a city truck." Wally laughed as he headed for the alley behind the Good Day Café on Georgia Street.

The woman behind the counter waved to Wally as they entered the café. She brought two steaming mugs of coffee and engaged in friendly chatter before moving on to other customers.

Wally glanced at Nick as he sipped his coffee. "So … Nick Shane. I know your name from the sports section of the *Times Herald*. You had a nice couple of years at Vallejo High. You still playing baseball?"

"Yeah, I played the past two seasons for Stan McWilliams at Vallejo JC. Stan's talking to four-year schools, trying to set me up with a scholarship for my last two years."

Wally smiled. "Good for you, kid. I didn't think you'd be a lifer in the Street Department. What are you, nineteen? Twenty?"

"Twenty, sir." The *sir* slipped out before Nick could catch it.

"Oh, my. Twenty." Wally shook his head and stared at his cup. "What made you decide to apply with the city?"

"Gus is a family friend. More than that, really. My dad died four years ago. Gus has been like a father to me. I asked him for the job and he said okay, as long as it was temporary, just until I went back to school. He mentioned not being a lifer."

"What about the draft, Nick? You worried about this damn war?"

"Oh, yeah. But they've got the lottery now, and I got lucky. My group number is 250. They tell me it's not likely they'll get beyond group 200."

"And if they do?"

"If it gets close, I'll probably enlist. Navy, most likely. My dad was a twenty-year Navy man."

The conversation continued, and Nick was glad Gus had paired him with Wally Grover, an all-around class act.

They left the café through the rear entrance and made their way toward the truck. Wally drove out of the alley, made a couple of turns, and headed east on Virginia Street. Nick watched him shift smoothly through the gears with a skillful double-clutch.

"Ever drive truck, Nick?"

"No, never had the opportunity."

"You wanna drive?" Wally grinned in his direction.

"What? You mean now?"

"Sure. No time like the present. We'll switch at the next stop."

They halted for a pothole and after the patch was done, Nick climbed in behind the wheel. The long, floor-mounted gearshift required the classic *H* pattern. From first to second, Nick ground the gears loudly, a sound worse than a thousand fingernails on a blackboard. From second to third, it was the same story. He tried to mimic Wally's double-clutch move, but it didn't seem to help. In the meantime, Wally had a good laugh, which added to Nick's anxiety.

"Don't force it, kid. Just let it drop into gear, nice and easy."

Pedestrians on the sidewalk stopped to stare in the direction of the grinding noise as Nick rolled up the street. He was grateful to see a pothole ahead, a reason to stop and end the carnage. As Wally tossed one last shovelful of asphalt into the hole, Nick waited to lower the bed, his own shovel propped against the back of the cab. Wally finished, and Nick activated the lever. The bed came down with a soft hydraulic hiss, down to a snug fit against the cab, snapping the wooden handle of Nick's shovel at the midpoint.

"Forgot to tell you, Nick. Don't prop your shovel against the back of the cab." Wally couldn't contain his laughter.

The laughter went on and before long, Nick was laughing too, convinced he would have to commit every rookie mistake, learn every lesson the hard way. He tossed his broken shovel into the bed of the truck and climbed back in behind the wheel, embarrassed and a little concerned.

"You think Gus will be pissed off?" Nick glanced at Wally.

"Nah. You're not the first and you won't be the last. We'll swing by the yard and pick up another shovel.

By day's end, Nick was sure he'd filled a thousand potholes and consumed as many cups of coffee. He pulled into the corporation yard on Amador Street and parked the large dump truck in its assigned slot. He and Wally made their way toward the shed that housed the lockers, anxious to store their gear and head for home. Several groups of men walked ahead of them.

Wally snickered. "Nick, see the guy up there in the green cap? The one with the shovel over his shoulder?" He pointed to a man walking next to old Mike Bouchka.

"Yeah."

"That's Norm Runyon. Look how he's carrying the shovel. I've got two words for you: accident prone."

From behind Nick, a voice called out, "Hey, Norm!" Norm stopped and turned to his left. The shovel swung around and whacked Mike on the back of the head.

Mike let fly his classic line. "You rotten sonofabitch!"

Norm apologized profusely while all the witnesses laughed out loud. Old Mike was uninjured, thank God. It was a strange end to Nick's first day on the job.

3

It was a quiet Sunday evening at the Relay, a clean, well-run saloon on Maine Street near Wilson Park. Nick and his buddies, Jeff and Grady, sat at the bar nursing their beers, glancing from time to time at the television above the back bar where *The Ed Sullivan Show* was in progress. They each carried a well-made driver's license proclaiming they were of legal age, though no one bothered to ask as long as they didn't disturb the quiet ambience.

The trio had grown up together, living in the same neighborhood and attending the same schools. They'd been teammates and competitors through every level of youth sports in the city, beginning with sandlot baseball at age seven. Just three guys who loved each other like brothers, though they may not say it out loud. And like brothers, they'd survived everything from simple differences of opinion to outright fistfights.

No one could ever mistake them for brothers physically. Grady was a solid six-footer built like the linebacker he used to be, his black hair cut high and tight, military style, his light gray eyes intense and intimidating. Jeff was barely five nine, a reed-thin point guard, his blonde hair cut shoulder length, with soulful brown eyes that missed very little. Nick was a muscular six two, 180 pounds, his light brown hair generally in need of being brushed away from his dark blue eyes. They were as different as three guys could be, yet any one of them would lay down his life for the others.

Nick glanced at the TV screen. "Is it just me, or is the Sullivan show going down the tubes?"

Jeff agreed. "Yeah, if I have to watch Topo Gigio one more time, I'm gonna barf."

Grady added his two cents. "It's like you can turn off the sound and not miss anything."

They watched Sullivan bumble his way through an introduction.

"So, buddy, how's the new job?" Jeff elbowed Nick and smiled.

"It's good. Good bunch of guys. But I think I'm the only one under fifty." Nick laughed.

"What do they have you doing?" Grady signaled the bartender for another round.

"Pothole duty. Easy money, but kinda boring. I'd like to do something else."

"What's it been, a couple of weeks?" Grady shoved a few dollars across the bar as the beers arrived.

"Two weeks. I start week three tomorrow." It was quiet for a moment. Nick changed the subject. "Hey, Jeff, what's up with you and the draft? Didn't you say your lottery number was coming up?"

"Yeah. Shit, man. I don't know what to do. I should probably go enlist. At least then I'd get to choose." Jeff studied his beer. "What about you, Grady?"

"Hell, I went to enlist in the marines. They turned me down. Said I had a heart murmur, or some damn thing."

"What? A jock like you? How can that be?" Nick and Jeff had the same reaction. They stared at their friend.

Grady shook his head. "I don't know. I need to go see a real doctor. Pissed me off. My dad was a marine. My grandfather was a marine. I'm ready to go, man. Kill me some commies."

"Come on, Grady." Nick turned toward his friend, incredulous. "Look at that damn war. Half the country thinks it was a mistake. Do you really think Nixon and Kissinger know what the hell they're doing? Any more than Johnson and McNamara?"

"Hey, if Vietnam goes, then it's gonna be Laos, Cambodia, Thailand. We've gotta stop the communists somewhere." Grady's voice rose, his neck turned red.

Nick and Jeff were quiet. They knew better than to push Grady. He was a hawk, it was in his genes, and there was no way to sway him.

Jeff broke the silence. "Look at what happened at Kent State last month. Can you believe it? Four students killed, nine wounded, and some just walking past the demonstration."

"Yeah, well, they were asking for it." Other customers glanced in Grady's direction now. "That was no demonstration. It was a riot. Throwing shit at the guardsmen. They're supposed to be students. They should get their asses to class."

"Okay, buddy. Calm down. Let's talk about something else, all right?" Nick had come to the Relay to relax, not fight.

Grady looked around. "Yeah, okay. Let's drop it." He turned to stare straight ahead, quiet for a moment.

Jeff tried a new direction. "So, Nick, how are things with you and Donna?"

"Good, I guess. I mean, we're fine. It's just, you know, she was accepted at UCLA. She'll be leaving in August for the fall semester."

"Wow! Good for her. She was always the smartest girl in our class. But damn, buddy, what are you gonna do with her down in L.A.?"

Nick had no answer, and so he tried a joke. "Well, maybe I could go fill potholes for the City of Angels."

"Hey, McWilliams is still working on a scholarship for you, right? Maybe he'll get you a ride to UCLA? Or some other school down there." Jeff sounded hopeful.

"Yeah, that would be great." Nick was wistful, wondering if he should call Coach McWilliams to check in, see if there was any progress.

Ed Sullivan said goodnight, and the three friends headed for the door. Tomorrow was a workday. For Nick, that meant more potholes to fill.

4

I n his dream, Nick was standing in the corporation yard, surrounded by the entire Street Department crew, holding a brand-new Mickey Mouse lunchbox. The men doubled over with laughter, pointing and slapping their knees, as Nick turned several shades of red. He woke with a start and looked at the clock on his bedside table. Five fifty. The alarm would sound at six. He closed his eyes and tried to return to sleep, minus the dream, when a familiar aroma drifted into the room.

Pancakes!

Nick threw back the covers and headed for the bathroom. From there, he dressed for work and went into the kitchen, where his mom stood over the old cast-iron griddle, about to remove four hotcakes to a waiting platter. Nick squeezed her shoulders and kissed her cheek.

"Good morning, gorgeous. Man, that smells good."

Lucille Shane smiled. "Have a seat, honey. They're coming off the griddle now." At sixty, her hair had gone snow white. Her thick, wire-rimmed glasses couldn't hide sparkling blue eyes. At five feet seven, Lucille was considered tall, until her son began to tower over her. She removed the four cakes, poured fresh batter onto the sizzling griddle, and then placed the platter on the table. Real butter and warm maple syrup were waiting, along with a steaming mug of coffee. Nick dug in.

"Nick, I packed two chicken sandwiches for you with some chips, an apple, and a couple of cookies. Is that enough?"

"Yeah, that's great." He wiped his mouth with a napkin. "Mom, you've been packing Dad's old lunch pail for me. You sure it's okay if I use it?"

"It's fine with me, honey, if you don't mind that beat-up old thing. We could get you a new one."

Nick laughed. "No, I don't mind. Matter of fact, I wanted to say thank you." He picked up his plate and headed for the sink to rinse it. Thank God for that old black lunch box. The Mickey Mouse theme played in his head and he smiled. He paused to look out the kitchen window as the sky lightened in the east.

How many times had Nick seen his father, Nick Sr., come home from work, that old tin box in hand? And the times his mother had to help his father take off his boots. His dad's back was so bad toward the end that he couldn't bend to take them off himself. Stay home? Take a sick day? That was out of the question. "I'm a working man," his father would say. That's all the explanation required. "I'm a working man." It's what he knew, all he knew: how to work harder than the next guy, harder than the next two guys combined.

Nick Sr. was a boilermaker, a trade he'd learned in the Navy, and he took pride in his craft. "Learn a trade, Nick. Nobody can take that away from you." Nobody, especially the bosses in their suits and ties, their polished wing-tip shoes, their manicured fingernails that never got dirty. "A working man has two things going for him, Nick. His union and the Democratic Party. Never forget that." Cross a union picket line? Never. Vote for a Republican? You've got to be kidding. And then, not long before he died, Nick Sr. said, "Stay in school, Nick. I don't want you to end up on that damn shipyard."

Learn a trade. Stay in school. Nick wasn't sure how to reconcile the two. What would his father think of Nick's job, humping a shovel with the Street Department for $395 a month? Would he be proud now that those new boots were a little dirty, some asphalt ground into the white soles? No, Nick knew he wasn't there, not yet. He didn't deserve to carry that lunch pail. There was more to do, more to prove. Nick wanted to make his father proud, and he would know when it happened. He'd look in the mirror one day and his old man would be there, a smile on his tired face and these words on his lips: "You're a working man, son."

He picked up the lunch pail and started for the front door, stopping to kiss his mother's cheek one more time. "I'm going to work, Mom. See you tonight."

Nick had been on the job three weeks. He was tired of pothole duty. It was time for some real work. He would have a talk with Gus.

5

Nick held the large platter while Gus Cordeiro scooped burgers from the barbeque grill with a long metal spatula. Gus switched to tongs to remove a half dozen hot dogs. They headed for the picnic table on the patio where Gerry, Gus's wife, was placing a large bowl of potato salad. The table was loaded with everything you could want on your burger or dog, plus steaming corn on the cob. Nick's girlfriend, Donna, came out of the kitchen with a large pitcher of lemonade and found an open spot for it. Nick smiled. He'd never left the Cordeiros' table hungry.

"Nick, there's beer in the cooler. Bring me one while you're at it." Gus motioned toward a large Coleman ice chest as he took his seat at the head of the table. Nick brought two ice-cold cans of Budweiser and handed one to Gus. "So, young man, you've been on the job three weeks. What do you think so far?"

"It's been great, Gus. Wally is a good guy. Really interesting life, with the Seabees and all."

"Yeah, he's a real artist with that damn grader, the best I've ever seen. I hope he doesn't decide to retire on me. He'll be a hard one to replace." Gus shook his head and looked at Nick. "How are you getting along with the rest of the guys? I hear they've named you Boots." He laughed.

"Hey, I don't mind. They're a good bunch."

"I tell you what, Nick, if they're jokin' with you, givin' you a hard time, it means they like you. It's when they stop that you gotta worry."

Nick smiled. "Yeah. I just want to show 'em I can carry my weight. Know what I mean?"

"Don't worry, Nick. You'll get plenty of chances for that."

Gerry and Donna ignored the men, deep into their own conversation. The two women had hit it off from the beginning, despite the age difference, when Nick had introduced Donna to the Cordeiros. Donna was polite and well-mannered, and it didn't take long to recognize her intelligence and confidence. And she was as pretty as she was smart. No question, Donna Foxworth was special.

The Cordeiros' sons, Gordon and Gus Jr., ages nine and twelve, joined them at the table, bringing their unique world of chaos and sibling rivalry. Gus and Gerry took turns attempting to enforce order, to little or no effect. Nick adored the boys, like two little brothers he wished he had.

It was July, and in Vallejo that meant cool, breezy evenings once the sun dipped low. They took dessert and coffee inside, the lively conversations continuing. Nick had a favor to ask. He waited until Gus poured a second cup of coffee.

"I've been doing potholes for three weeks now, Gus. How about moving me to the paving crew? I'd like to do some real work, break a sweat, get my hands dirty."

Gus rubbed his forehead and glanced at Nick. "My paving teams are set right now. But I tell you what: I'm shorthanded on the painting crew. How 'bout that?"

Nick wasn't crazy about the idea, but he was bored with pothole detail. Anything would be a step up. And so it was set: Mike would go back to Wally, and Nick would learn about painting. It wouldn't hurt to splash some paint on those new boots.

Nick and Donna said goodbye to the Cordeiros around 7:30. They drove west along Georgia Street, heading toward downtown, no destination in mind.

"It's still early. How about a movie?" Nick glanced at Donna, snuggled close to him on the front seat. "I think *True Grit* is playing at the El Rey."

"I've got a better idea." She smiled at him. "Morgan is out of town with her boyfriend. I have the key to her apartment."

"Really? Do you think she'd mind?"

"No … not if we change the bedding afterward." She looked at him and smiled again.

"Geez, does she think we're funky or something? Like we're gonna stink up the bed?" He was laughing now.

Donna rested her head on his shoulder. "We're all funky, sweetie. No big deal. We'll change the sheets."

Nick sped up a little, heading for the old, converted fourplex up on Napa Street.

Nick stared at the ceiling, stroking Donna's short brown hair. Her head rested on his chest, her body half over his. Nick's heart was full. He waited for the lump in his throat to clear.

"Donna, what's going to happen?"

"What do mean, sweetie?"

"I mean to us. You and me."

"Well, I hope what just happened happens again … soon. That was wonderful." She laughed softly.

"Be serious. You know what I mean."

"I thought we agreed. It's settled. We're not gonna talk about it again."

"I can't help it, Donna. I love you. I want to be with you. I'd marry you tomorrow—"

She scooted up onto the pillow and turned to face him. "Come on, Nick. We've talked about this. I've been accepted at UCLA, I leave in August for my junior year. When I get my undergrad, I'm going to apply to medical schools. I'm going to be a doctor, Nick, no matter what it takes. That's a lot of years, and marriage doesn't figure in the plan right now."

"I know, but—"

"And what about you? You're going to be off playing baseball somewhere. We're likely to be thousands of miles apart."

Nick was quiet, searching her eyes. God, why did he have to fall for a girl with a ten-year plan—and the brains and guts to make it happen?

"Look, Nickie. You've told me how you feel when you're on a ball field, how you come alive inside."

"Yeah …"

"Well, that's how I feel about school, about learning, about becoming a doctor. Understand?"

Nick had no arguments, or at least none that made sense. She was right about his love of the game. If she felt that way about her goals, how could he get in the way? He pulled her to him and held her close. It was July, and she wouldn't be leaving until August. He was not ready to let her go.

6

Ralph Berger managed the painting crew. As of this Monday morning in July, that crew numbered just two: Ralph and Nick. Ralphie, as everyone called him, was in his late fifties and stood about five six with his boots on. His florid complexion gave away his love of good whiskey, which he carried in a silver flask in the back pocket of his white coveralls. Drinking on the job never seemed to impair his skill with the tools of the trade. Whether painting posts, crosswalks, curbs, or warning signs, Ralphie kept a steady hand.

Nick liked him right away. For one thing, the conversation never lagged because Ralphie never shut up. An endless stream of anecdotes filled the day, ranging from Ralph's childhood on the Near West Side of Chicago, to his service in the Army during World War II, and on to his current life in Vallejo. All Nick had to do was ask a leading question.

"What's Chicago like, Ralph?"

"Oh, great town, Boots. You'd love it. You got the great museums, the aquarium, the zoos, the Art Institute. You're a baseball guy, you've got the Sox and the Cubs. And there's the Bears, the Bulls, the Blackhawks. Great sports town, Boots."

A converted ammunition carrier dating from the forties served as the paint truck. A large tank mounted in the bed fed a fifty-foot hose for spraying crosswalks and traffic warnings. Brushes, rollers, paint buckets, thinners, and rags filled the rest of the bed. Ralphie ran a tight ship: a place for everything and everything in its place, including a fifth of Old Kessler to refill his flask. The crew set out early with a long list of jobs to complete. Ralph continued his narrative.

"Ever hear of Maxwell Street? My old man had a stall on Maxwell. Sold clothing, whatever he could get his hands on, bought from some of the best stores in the Loop when they were clearing out for a new season. He'd pick up good stuff for pennies on the dollar, mark it up, and make a nice profit. Of course, a lot of his stuff 'fell off the truck,' if you know what I mean. 'Fell off the truck.' Ha! But hell, if you went up and down Maxwell, half the goods you'd see were off somebody's truck. And there were food carts all along the street, Boots. The smells were amazing, but the best was this cart that sold hot dogs. Ever had a Chicago hot dog, kid?"

"No, can't say I have." No question: Nick was going to hear all about Chicago hot dogs.

They stopped to paint a crosswalk, laying out the stencils, painting one lane at a time, and waiting for the paint to dry before moving on. From there, a couple of stop signs with posts in need of paint, and then more crosswalks. The list of jobs seemed endless.

"You've got to start with a good all-beef frank, Boots. Vienna is the best. Gotta be Vienna. You boil it for ten minutes or so, nothing fancy, and then you gotta have a steamed poppy-seed bun—without a doubt the best, gotta be poppy-seed. So, you've got your dog, your bun, and now you gotta have good yellow mustard. And don't even think about catsup. No self-respecting Chicagoan would put catsup on a hot dog. So, yellow mustard, and then the relish—and it's gotta be the bright green relish that you see in the Midwest, not this pale-lookin' stuff they have out here."

At the base of the Georgia Street hill, the intersection with Amador, they prepared to paint STOP followed by AHEAD in the eastbound lane approaching the corner. Ralph put down the stencils while Nick set out barricades and traffic cones to divert traffic. Ralph returned to the tale of the Chicago hot dog.

"So, you got the dog, bun, mustard, and relish. Now you gotta have a nice ripe tomato, and you put two or three slices, stuff 'em right in the bun. And a yellow onion, you can either slice some crescents or dice 'em up. Then a sprinkle of celery salt, and finally you top it with a kosher dill pickle spear. I'm tellin' you, Boots, that's a meal on a bun, and this cart down on Maxwell was the best in Chicago. And don't even get me started on the Polish sausage."

Ralph unrolled the hose and sprayed white paint into the stencil. He'd completed STOP and was starting on AHEAD when Joe Jacoby, the department foreman, pulled to the curb in his pickup truck. Joe was Gus's right-hand man, and they complemented each other so well that Joe could finish Gus's sentences (and often did). Joe was a tall, lean man with a perpetual smile and a new joke to tell at every meeting. Ralph and Nick paused to greet him.

"Ralphie, Boots. How's it going? Hey, did you guys hear the one about the traveling salesman who ran over the farmer's cat?" Joe was off and running while he inspected their progress. They all laughed at the punch line, but Joe wasn't finished. "Holy moly! Ralph, look at what you're doin' here."

"What? What's the problem?" Ralph reached for his flask but stopped short.

"Damn, Ralph! You're painting it upside down." Joe's smile revealed tobacco-stained teeth. "A driver has to read it heading east." He pointed dramatically, like a referee signaling a first down. "Eastbound, Ralphie."

"Ah, shit!" Ralph's face turned bright red.

"And you, Joe College …" Jacoby turned to Nick. "Where were you? You just let him go ahead and do it?" The foreman threw back his head and howled with laughter. "Okay, look. Get your black paint, paint out what you've got, and start over. And for chrissakes, get it right this time." He turned and headed for his truck, laughing all the way.

Ralph went to the paint truck and sat down on the running board. He pulled his flask and took a long swig.

"Damn, Boots! It's gonna be hard livin' this one down."

"You don't think Joe will say anything, do you?"

Ralph shook his head. "Kid, we are about to be famous."

Nick couldn't hold it any longer. He started to laugh, and it was a long time before he could stop.

The sun was low in the west as they turned into the corporation yard, drove to the paint shed, and started the process of cleaning brushes, rollers, and nozzles. Ralph was right: the word had spread through the crew like a prairie fire. Trucks rolled into the yard with guys hanging out of windows and yelling, "Hey, Ralph! Eastbound, Ralphie, eastbound!"

And Nick learned he had a new nickname. He was Joe College.

7

oaches and scouts referred to Nick Shane as a late bloomer. In high school, he'd been something of a runt, five nine with his spikes on, 165 pounds with a pocketful of pennies. He'd performed well, carrying a .400 average during his senior season. And yet the scouts looked at his small stature and went off to seek other prospects. Nick could run, field, and hit, but his throwing arm was unimpressive, and he had little power with the bat. He was a three-tool guy when the gold standard required five tools—run, throw, field, hit, and hit with power. No college recruiters or pro scouts came calling at the Shane residence.

That began to change during his two years at Vallejo Junior College. Nick experienced a growth spurt. He reached six feet and then six two. His weight climbed to 180 pounds and it was solid muscle. The hours he spent in the weight room made sure of that. Fly balls that barely reached the warning track began to leave the yard. Scouts took notice, and yet old opinions persisted. Nick remained a *maybe*, a guy to *watch and see*, a possible *roster filler*.

Stan McWilliams, his coach at Vallejo JC, had promised to set Nick up with a scholarship offer. Nick tried to keep his hopes alive as the summer of '70 wore on. To hone his skills, he played weekend games with the Vallejo Builders, a semipro team that was part of the North Bay League, a loose affiliation of teams from cities around the Bay Area: Napa, Vacaville, San Rafael, San Francisco, Berkeley, Oakland. The players ranged from young hopefuls like Nick to middle-aged veterans and former professionals, the kids hoping to be noticed and the older guys clinging to the game they loved.

The sun was bright in the Northern California sky, temperatures in the low eighties. A light breeze out of the west pushed puffy white clouds over Wilson Park in Vallejo. The Builders were set to play the San Francisco Seals on this Saturday afternoon in August, the first game of a home-and-home matchup that would conclude on Sunday in San Francisco.

Nick sprinted from the dugout to his position in center field. He never got over the charge he felt at the start of every game. His legs were coiled steel springs, his glove a vacuum to suck up any ball hit his way, his arm a cannon to gun down base runners. The umpire shouted, "Play ball!" precisely at 1:05 p.m., and a simple thought raced through Nick's mind: *Hit it to me. I dare you. Hit it to me.*

It happened in the top of the sixth inning with the score tied, two to two. Sal Barboni, first baseman for the Seals—all six feet four, 260 pounds of him—connected with a fastball and sent it soaring toward left-center field. Would it clear the chain-link fence more than four hundred feet away? The answer from the hundred or so fans in attendance was, *Tell it goodbye.*

Nick had another answer in mind. With the crack of the bat, he made a neat drop-step and raced back and to his right, every ounce of strength and energy poured into the effort. The spectators sat, mouths open, holding their collective breath with the realization that Nick was gaining on the ball. He actually had a chance. His left arm extended with one final lunge, and the ball stuck in his glove as he slammed into the fence. The thick wire fabric caught his body like a trampoline and sent him bouncing back onto the field, the ball in his glove held high for the umpire to see.

For Sal Barboni, it was a long, loud out.

The Builders went on to defeat the Seals in the first game of the weekend series. A handful of scouts were in attendance, there to see other players. They jotted notes about Nick's performance on three-by-five cards and scraps of paper.

Doesn't look like the N. Shane we scouted in high school. Could deserve another look.

Plays the game with a perpetual smile. Great attitude!

Maybe we missed this guy. (Wouldn't be the first.)

Don Gleason, a reporter for the *Vallejo Times Herald,* filed this story for the Sunday morning sports page:

Builders defeat Seals 5-3 at Wilson Park

Through all the years of covering local baseball teams, this reporter has never witnessed a play like the one turned in yesterday by Nick Shane. A real game-changer!

The box score accompanying the article showed that Nick had four at bats, scored two runs, had two hits, and was credited with three runs-batted-in. An all-around good day down at the ballyard. But the report didn't mention the visitor Nick received in the dugout after the game.

Nick was busy packing his equipment bag when the man came down the steps into the dugout. Large and heavy-set, with a friendly smile on his face, he reached out to Nick with a hand the size of a catcher's mitt.

"Nick Shane? Hi, I'm Dante Benedetti. I sponsor the team you just beat." Nick stood to shake hands. Benedetti continued. "Nice game today. That was some catch!"

"Thank you, sir. Got a little lucky, I guess." Nick recognized the name. Dante Benedetti was known as Mr. Baseball in San Francisco. He was the owner of a well-known North Beach restaurant, and he sponsored teams from Little League through semipro. He was reported to be a friend of the DiMaggio brothers.

"Will you be coming to the city for tomorrow's game?"

"Yes, sir. I wouldn't miss it." Nick smiled, warming to this friendly celebrity.

"Tell me, son, what are your plans? What comes after the Vallejo Builders?"

Nick paused, surprised by the question. "Well, my JC coach is trying to line up a scholarship for me. I want to finish my degree, major in education, become a teacher." He looked at the older man for a reaction. "That's about it, for now."

"That's a good goal. Good for you, Nick."

"Why do you ask, sir?" Nick felt his cheeks flush. Was he being too direct?

"Let's just say I know a guy who knows a guy." Benedetti laughed. "Let's talk again tomorrow. Okay?"

"Sure." Nick took the large hand that was offered and shook it firmly.

I know a guy who knows a guy? Sunday would be an interesting day.

8

"So, this Mr. Benedetti, what did he say?" Donna looked up, waiting for Nick's answer.

"Turns out he knows a guy at the University of Virginia in Charlottesville. He's working with Coach McWilliams, setting up a campus visit for me."

"That's great, Nick! When do you go?"

"Sometime in September or October. If they offer a scholarship, I need to sign a letter of intent in early November. I'd start classes there in August of '71, about a year from now. It's still a big *if*."

Nick and Donna relaxed on the couch in Morgan's apartment while Morgan and her boyfriend, Zeke, were busy in the kitchen putting the final touches on dinner. The apartment was an odd configuration resulting from the conversion of an old, two-story Victorian. The front door opened into a living room with high ceilings and bright white walls. The living room gave way to the bedroom, what had once been the dining room of the old mansion.

Pocket doors could be closed to provide privacy but were seldom used. A door at the back of the bedroom led to a large kitchen big enough for a dining table and six chairs, in addition to the sink and the appliances. In one corner of the room, near the door to the bedroom, a full bath had been added. Morgan referred to the floor plan as the Mystery House, but somehow it worked. The landlord had maintained the apartment well and furnished it with sturdy but inexpensive pieces.

Morgan called from the kitchen to tell them dinner was ready. The table was set with a large platter of spaghetti and meatballs, green salad, crusty sourdough bread, and a basket-covered bottle of Chianti. The four friends sat down to the sumptuous feast.

Zeke made sure wine glasses were full and then raised his own. "Here's to Donna, leaving tomorrow for UCLA. Donna, we wish you all the best. And the next time we do this, let it be a toast to Doctor Donna Foxworth." They touched glasses, drank their wine, and filled their plates.

The toast hit Nick like a punch to the heart. Donna was leaving in the morning, her parents driving her to Los Angeles to check into her dorm. This would be their last night together. Nick tried to put it out of his mind by joining the spirited conversation.

After dinner, Morgan and Zeke insisted on doing the dishes. Nick and Donna returned to the couch in the front room. The latest issue of *Playboy* magazine lay on the coffee table. Nick picked it up and opened the centerfold.

"Whoa! That's an interesting pose."

Donna laughed. "You guys like that stuff, don't you?"

"Nah. Too much makeup." Nick put on a frown.

"Oh, as if you're looking at her face."

"Hey, Donna, you could do this … be a *Playboy* model."

"Ha! No way. I'm barely a C-cup. These girls are all Ds. Maybe double-D."

"Yeah but look at this feature. 'Girls of the Southeast Conference.' College girls. Maybe they'll do 'Girls of the Pacific Coast Conference.' You could represent UCLA."

"Very funny. For one thing, my father would kill me."

Morgan and Zeke emerged from the kitchen, Morgan carrying her purse and a light jacket.

"Okay, lovebirds. Zeke and I are meeting some friends for drinks and a movie. We'll be gone for two or three hours. Make yourselves at home, if you know what I mean." She laughed, but then her voice changed. "Donna, give me hug, sweet girl."

Donna jumped up to hug her friend. They held each other close. "Don't cry, Morgan. I'll be home for Thanksgiving. And I'll call you. Okay? Soon as I get settled."

Morgan broke away, wiped her eyes, and headed out the front door with Zeke. "Lock up when you leave, sweetie." They hurried down the steps. "And remember to change the sheets." Morgan's laughter faded as she headed toward Zeke's car at the curb.

"Well that was subtle." Nick chuckled as he closed the front door.

"Yeah, well, we've got a couple of hours, lover. Let's make 'em count." Donna turned and headed for the bedroom.

Nick shook his head in wonder. *God, what a girl! How am I gonna live without her?*

It happened at the worst conceivable moment. They heard a commotion at the front door—keys jingled, doorknob rattled, tires screeched as a car tore away from the curb. Morgan burst into the living room. She threw her purse on the couch, kicked off her shoes, and ran for the bedroom, where she dove onto the bed. Nick and Donna barely had time to separate. Morgan sobbed hysterically as Donna gathered her in her arms.

"That Zeke is such an asshole. I hate him! I hate him, Donna. I never want to see him again. He's such an asshole …" Morgan went on, tears and rage out of control. Her breath reeked of alcohol. Drinks with friends had not gone well.

Nick retrieved his clothes from the foot of the bed and tried to sneak away to the bathroom.

"Ooo, nice butt, Nickie!" Morgan shouted after him. She giggled for a moment but then dissolved in tears again.

Nick dressed while Donna did her best to comfort Morgan. He went into the kitchen and started a pot of coffee. It might be a long night. A while later, Donna and Morgan joined him around the kitchen table. Morgan was in the midst of describing Zeke's asshole-ness—something about flirting in public with another girl—when they heard a loud knock at the front door. Nick went to answer. It was Zeke in a state of emotional meltdown.

"Nick, geez, I've gotta talk to Morgan. Let me in, man."

"Not a good idea, Zeke. She doesn't want to see you right now."

"Come on, man. I've got to talk to her, to apologize." He started through the door.

Nick placed his hand on Zeke's chest and held him in the doorway. "Zeke, I'm telling you, this is not a good time. You need to leave."

Zeke looked past Nick and shouted into the apartment. "Morgan! Morgan, I'm sorry, baby. I messed up, I know it. I'm sorry—"

Morgan shouted from the kitchen. "Go away, Zeke! Get outta here. I never wanna see you again."

"I love you, Morgan! I love you, baby. I swear to God, I'm sorry. Morgan!"

Nick saw a streak of light and color as Morgan rushed past him and into Zeke's arms, the two of them sobbing and apologizing at once. Their embrace morphed into a passionate make-out session.

Nick and Donna looked at each other and shrugged. They gathered their things and left quietly, shutting the door behind them.

Nick held the car door open for Donna. "Oops."

"What?" Donna looked up as she entered the vehicle.

"We didn't change the sheets."

It felt good to share a laugh.

Nick was quiet as he drove across town, taking Donna home. Maybe it had been a good thing, all the drama with Morgan and Zeke. No time for tears and regrets. Nick tried to count the days until Thanksgiving when Donna would be home. He gave up, sure of only one thing: it was a hell of a long time.

9

All through the Steffan Manor neighborhood, sidewalks were set six feet inside the curb. Along the six-foot-wide curb strip, the city had planted sycamore trees, now nearly thirty years old. The roots of the mature trees lifted and broke the sidewalks and curbs, creating an ongoing task for the Street Department. The broken concrete had to be taken out with a jackhammer, the offending roots cut back, and new sections of concrete poured.

The work began promptly at eight, heading up the Laurel Street hill from the intersection with Buss Street. A member of the crew with a fifty-pound jackhammer began to break the old concrete into chunks. As he moved along the walk, followed by the large compressor mounted on a trailer at curbside, men would jump in to take the chunks and toss them onto the street, where a front-loader would scoop up the debris and drop it into a dump truck.

After the old concrete was cleared away, men with axes would go to work on the protruding tree roots, and when they were finished, another crew would come with two-by-fours and metal stakes to frame for new curb and sidewalk. Later in the day, a truck would show up to pour concrete into the frames, followed by the finishers with their rakes, trowels, and brooms.

This little army made its way up Laurel Street from tree to tree, section to section, each crew performing its given task. Nick's job: lift the chunks of concrete and toss them to the street, then take an axe to the tree roots. It was backbreaking work, and it felt good.

The noon whistle sounded on the shipyard five miles to the west. The men found a shady spot on the curb strip and opened their lunch pails. Nick was finishing his lunch and chatting with his mates when their crew leader, Ed Martin, approached.

"Hey, Joe College, I hear you want to try your hand with the jackhammer." Ed gave him a skeptical grin.

"Yeah, Ed. Can you check me out, show me what to do?"

"Sure, kid. Come with me."

Nick closed his lunch pail and followed Martin up the street. The compressor, quiet for the moment, waited at the curb, the jackhammer leaned against a sycamore. Ed Martin lifted the tool and carried it like a toy to a cracked section of sidewalk.

"Okay, this lever on the right handle activates the bit. Just plant the bit where you want it and let the tool do the work. Give it your weight, but don't try to force it. When you lift it, bend your knees like this, hold the hammer close to your thighs, and lift with your legs. If you try horsing it around with your arms, you'll ruin your back. Just take your time and let the tool do the work. And for God's sake, keep your toes out of the way. Got it?"

"Got it. Thanks, Ed." *Seems easy enough. I'm twenty years old and a damn fine athlete. Hell, I can handle a jackhammer.*

Ed gave Nick a pair of overshoes with steel toes to slip over his boots, then handed him a pair of clear safety goggles. Class was over; time to go back to work. Ed started the engine on the compressor that fed the thick orange hose connected to the jackhammer. Nick set the bit firmly on the damaged sidewalk and squeezed the lever. The noise, the pounding, and the shaking racked his body, and he nearly lost his balance. He reset the bit and squeezed the lever again. Same result. Nick looked up to see a half-dozen guys watching and laughing as he fought the machine. He'd show them.

Go ahead and laugh, assholes. You'll never see me quit.

By midafternoon, Nick had broken up the last section of sidewalk on Laurel Street and secured the jackhammer on the truck that pulled the compressor. Ed Martin clapped a hand on Nick's shoulder.

"Good work, kid. Come with me. We've got one more quick job to do."

They engaged in small talk as they drove across town, heading toward South Vallejo. It was quiet for moment and Nick was curious about the *quick job.*

"Where are we going, Ed?"

"To Mike Bouchka's place. We have some asphalt left over from a job and we're gonna fix his driveway."

"Is Gus okay with this?" Nick looked out the window at Wilson Park as they headed southwest.

"Well, let's just say Joe Jacoby did the estimating and Gus signed the order." Ed laughed and turned into a residential neighborhood just off Sonoma Boulevard. Several city trucks were parked up the street near a neat two-story house. "This is Mike's place, Nick. I need you to break up the old asphalt with the jackhammer. We've got a different bit to use. I'll help you change it."

The driveway in front of Mike's home was twenty feet long and about the same width. Half of the driveway, connecting to the street, was paved in asphalt. The rest, leading into the garage, was concrete. The crew stood by to replace the worn and rutted asphalt. Nick helped Ed change the bit on the jackhammer to a flat blade.

Ed fired up the compressor, and Nick went to work. He finished in about thirty minutes.

Nick and Ed stowed the jackhammer as the crew cleared away the old pavement and smoothed and tamped the base. A truck pulled forward towing a trailer with a stinking, oil-covered tank. A hose connected to a long wand was unrolled, and a black oily substance sprayed over the subsurface. Ed explained that it was a tack coat, intended to bond the new asphalt to the base. With that task completed, a truck backed into position and dumped new asphalt into the prepared space. Men jumped in to spread the material, tossing it expertly with their shovels. Everyone stood back as a guy named Don, an expert with the long-handled aluminum rake, leveled the surface to near-perfection. When Don signaled his satisfaction, a large diesel roller with two steel drums for wheels moved in to finish the job, rolling back and forth over the surface. They all stepped back to admire the work, which from start to finish took little more than an hour.

While this activity was underway, old Mike stood off to the side. Next to him, a short, gray-haired woman with a sweet smile held his left hand. The men addressed her as Dory or Mrs. Bouchka. As the work finished, she spoke to two men who went into the garage and returned with a case of ice-cold beer. Dory Bouchka invited everyone to enjoy a tall, cold one and then went through the crew, clasping hands and saying thanks. Nick smiled as she reached for his hand.

"Oh, my," she said. "You are a young one. Thank you. Thank you so much for this."

The five o'clock whistle blew on the shipyard. The men finished their beer and headed for home base.

"How do you feel, Nick? Long day, eh?" Ed Martin grinned at him as they cruised along Sonoma Boulevard.

Nick's thoughts were with old Mike Bouchka and his sweet wife. "What? Oh, yeah. I'm gonna sleep well tonight."

STREET CRED

He flexed his aching shoulders and glanced at the older man next to him. Ed hadn't called him Joe College or Boots since they'd broken for lunch. Maybe he'd accomplished something this day.

10

Nick downshifted as they began the climb out of Jenner, heading north on Highway 1. The V-8 rumbled smoothly, more than up to the challenge of the winding road. The early morning air was cool, and they'd left the top up on the old Ford convertible. Now they rolled down the windows to savor the breeze off the Pacific, the pungent mixture of saltwater and kelp.

The road rose and fell and rose again, clinging to the cliffs overlooking the rugged coast. They came to a point where the highway crossed a long flat ridge, and there to the north, Ft. Ross came into view. It was a pretty picture: the rectangular walls of the old stockade surrounding the few remaining buildings, the Russian Orthodox chapel built of redwood standing proudly in the southeast corner. It was a welcome sight because it meant they were only a few minutes from their destination.

Nick, Jeff, and Grady were headed for a cove just north of Ft. Ross, a spot where enduring memories had been made. They'd first visited the cove as twelve-year-olds, camping and fishing with Grady's parents. That trip had been epic, resulting in a washtub full of fish—black and red snapper, sea trout, cabezon, even a couple of ling cod. They'd been back many times, and though the catch had been adequate, it never came close the level of that first visit. Yet the beauty of the place drew them again and again.

With the fort behind them as they approached from the south, the highway made a graceful curve to embrace the cove. Nick slowed, checked for cars in either direction, and then made a quick U-turn to park on the west side of the highway. A wide patch of ground allowed ample room off the southbound lane.

A well-worn path led down the steep cliff to the narrow beach. At the north end of the beach, a freshwater stream flowed out of a redwood canyon, washing the base of a great rock that sat at the water's edge. A hike up the canyon was like entering a cathedral, sunlight streaming down through the redwoods, each bend in the stream presenting a view more beautiful than the last.

Once upon a time, the cove had been the sight of a timbering operation. Until the early sixties, a massive incinerator, looking like a tall, rusted wigwam, sat up on the cliff above the north point. The boys had always known this place as Timber Cove, though it was a mile or two south of the lodge bearing that name.

And here they were, one more time. It was a farewell adventure for Jeff, who had been drafted and would be leaving soon for basic training. They climbed out of the car and approached the edge of the cliff, looking down on the familiar scene.

"It never changes. Thank God." Nick loved this cove, his favorite place on the planet.

"Yeah. About the only change was when they tore down the incinerator." Grady took a deep breath and stretched, happy the two-hour ride from Vallejo was over.

"Let's get the stuff down to the beach and then get some fishing done, before the wind comes up." Jeff checked his watch. It was

7:00 a.m., a good time to get a line in the water. "We can set up camp later."

It took a couple of trips to get their gear down to the beach. They dropped everything at the north end near the creek, a spot that gave some protection from the wind that would come blasting from the northwest in the afternoon. They grabbed their fishing gear and the bait they'd purchased in Bodega Bay and headed for their favorite spot around the north point away from the beach, a rocky shelf that hung out over the surf. The three friends smiled while they rock-hopped their way, as though heading for the promised land.

The morning bite wasn't bad—six fish for the large cooler. They took a break for lunch and then set up camp. The nine-by-twelve tent would provide shelter from wind and fog, and the two-burner stove was more than adequate to heat large cans of Dinty Moore beef stew for dinner. Nick made a quick trip up the road to a small grocery to buy ice for the fish and the beer. Then it was time for a hike up the canyon to see what changes time had wrought.

Back in camp, they rested, waiting for the afternoon wind to subside. Then it was back to north point, to that rock shelf over the surf, for the evening bite. They reeled in five more snappers—three red, two black—to toss in the cooler.

Time now to watch the sun dive into the Pacific, a magnificent display of yellow and orange. Wood gathered from the beach and the canyon fed a small campfire, the firepit formed by large rocks rolled into place. It was a day to remember. Good fishing, fine August weather, and great company.

"Gentlemen, I have a little surprise for you." Nick went into his duffle, pulled out a fifth of Wild Turkey, and held it high. "To celebrate our pal Jeffrey, heading off to be a soldier."

Tin cups were filled, toasts were offered, and they settled back to enjoy the campfire, the cold beer, and the smooth sting of good whiskey.

"Jeff, tell me something, buddy. Why didn't you enlist like you planned? Why just accept the draft?" It was growing dark now. Nick could see Jeff's face, lit by the campfire.

"I don't know, man. It's like I couldn't move, like my feet were in cement. I wanted to do something, anything, to stay out of Vietnam. But I couldn't do it, couldn't pull the trigger."

"Hell, here I am, ready to go, and I can't get in." Grady couldn't contain his frustration.

"Grady, did you see a doc? Did he confirm your heart murmur?" Nick passed the bottle to Jeff.

"Yeah. What bullshit. I'm in better shape than 90 percent of the guys going to Vietnam, I guarantee it." Grady shook his head. "What about you, Nick? Anybody at the draft board been in touch?"

"Nope. But they know where to find me."

It was quiet for a while. Nick looked up to the heavens and admired the Milky Way, always amazed at how many stars were visible out here away from civilization. His thoughts turned to another perfect night spent here at the cove.

"I brought Donna here once. I think we pitched the tent in this same spot."

Grady and Jeff took in that thought and mulled it over, along with their whiskey.

"Man, you are one lucky guy, Nick." Jeff smiled and raised his cup.

"Damn, you got that right." Grady joined the salute.

"Here's to Donna." Nick made it unanimous. "And to Jeff. Keep your head down and cast a short shadow."

They downed the whiskey, cooled their throats with ice cold beer, and threw another log on the fire.

11

Gus Cordeiro left Nick with these words of advice: "Bring old shoes if you've got 'em. The tack coat and the asphalt will ruin your good boots." Nick would start work with the paving crew on Tuesday, the day after Labor Day.

He climbed the stairs to the attic and found his father's old foot locker. He moved it away from its place against the wall and opened the lid. Nick's mom had placed a few items of clothing, laundered and carefully folded, in the locker. These were things that were too good or too precious to throw out: denim work pants, dark blue work shirts, an old gray fedora, and at the bottom of the stack a battered pair of boots wrapped in old newsprint. Nick lifted the boots from the locker and set them on the floor. The rubber heels were rounded, the neoprene soles smooth with wear. Would they fit? Dad was barely five nine, his shoes at least a size smaller than Nick's.

STREET CRED

Nick slipped on the right shoe. Not bad. The wear and tear had softened the leather, made it pliable. This would work. With his mom's approval, Nick had the old shoes Gus recommended.

September brought Indian summer to the North Bay, temperatures rising into the eighties and nineties. Nick remembered his back-to-school days at Vallejo High, shopping for Pendleton shirts and crew-neck sweaters, then letting them hang in the closet until Halloween. Now he'd be on the street rather than in a classroom, a different kind of education.

The assignment was a major repair along Tuolumne Street, running north from Tennessee. Wally Grover maneuvered the Caterpillar grader, cutting away the old asphalt and piling it to be loaded and hauled away. Nick and his mates jumped in to remove any loose debris. The foul-smelling oil truck came along to spray the tack coat over the base, followed by a large dump truck that dropped hot black asphalt in a long low heap. Now the shovel crew (Nick included) began to spread the material over the surface. It was midmorning, the temperature climbing. Sweat poured from arms and foreheads, and the men striped to T-shirts as they worked their way up the street. When the shovel work was done, they stood by while their man Don, the master of the long aluminum rake, smoothed the surface to near perfection. Then came Norm Runyon with the heavy roller, packing the surface to permanence.

Every truck carried a ten-gallon water jug and a supply of paper cups. Staying hydrated was a must. When the noon whistle blew, they'd completed the work as far as Illinois Street. The men found shady spots along the walk and opened their lunch pails. Joe Jacoby approached as Nick filled his mouth with turkey on wheat.

"How's it going, kiddo? Still havin' fun?"

"Oh, yeah, Joe. It's a blast."

"Look …" Joe lowered his voice. "I've been watching you. Pace yourself, okay? You don't have anything to prove out here." He flashed a smile.

"Got it, Joe. Thanks."

Joe turned to a group nearby. "So, this Irishman walks into his favorite pub, says to the bartender, 'Michael, me friend, did ya hear 'bout the new place over on Fifth Street? For five bucks, you get a pint, a free lunch, and they take ya in the back room and ya get laid.' Michael says, 'Ya don't say? And you've been to this place, Paddy?' Paddy says, 'No, but me girlfriend has.'" Joe soaked up the laughter and then went to check progress farther up the street.

Back at work after lunch, they finished a section and stood back for Norm to come with the roller. Nick was busy using his shovel to knock the caked oil and asphalt from the soles of his father's shoes when he heard voices shouting for Norm's attention.

"Norm! Hey, Norm!"

"Look out!"

"The tree—"

Norm was riding in the driver's seat atop the rear roller, his foot on the accelerator, his right hand manipulating the wishbone steering lever. He peered back over the roller to admire his handiwork. The diesel engine was too loud; he didn't hear the warnings. He turned his head just in time to raise his right arm in defense. The limb of a curbside tree caught him under the armpit and plucked him neatly off the seat. There he hung while the roller continued, coasting to a stop ten feet away. Nick and two others ran to where Norm dangled from the limb and grabbed his legs, easing him down to the pavement. Then the laughter started, and it seemed like it would never stop.

Another Norm Runyon classic.

Late in the day, the crew came to the intersection of Nebraska Street. Nick stood at the curb as Norm rolled the last section of pavement. Mike Bouchka shuffled to Nick's side and touched his elbow.

"Hey, Mike. How's it goin'?" Nick was surprised, not sure what to expect.

Mike smiled his lopsided smile. "I knew your old man."

"Really?"

"Legion Post 104. Both of us members." Mike formed the words carefully.

"I'll be darned. I didn't know that ... that you knew each other."

"We shot pool. He was a good stick." Mike smiled again. "Liked his beer too."

Nick laughed. "Oh, you got that right."

"Hard workin' sonofabitch, your old man."

"Yeah, that too."

"You're just like him." Mike reached with his left hand and squeezed Nick's forearm. He turned and shuffled away.

Nick stared at the pavement for a while and then smiled. It was the message he'd wanted to hear, but from an unexpected source. The five o'clock whistle blew on the shipyard. Time to head for home.

12

Nick cruised down I-405 heading for Los Angeles, the windows of the classic Ford Coupe rolled down, the radio cranked up. Diana Ross added to the beautiful fall day, singing "Ain't No Mountain High Enough." Nick sang along in his flat, out-of-tune tenor. This was his first trip to L.A., a last-minute, down-on-Saturday, back-on-Sunday whirlwind.

He had to see Donna.

Nick exited the freeway and headed east on Wilshire Boulevard. He followed the directions Donna provided and found a parking structure on the edge of the UCLA campus. The plan was to meet at the Bruin statue, easy for Nick to find.

Donna had proposed a long list of things to see and do. She walked toward him with a beautiful smile, and his heart leapt to his throat. God how he'd missed her. They embraced, and he held her till it began to attract attention. They kissed quickly, hugged again, and then Donna took his hand and led him on a tour of the campus.

"How was the drive? Was the traffic bad on the Grapevine? Did you eat on the way down? No? Good, we'll get some lunch …" Donna had an endless list of questions between pointing out major landmarks. "And this is Pauley Pavilion. You know we're NCAA Champions again this year. John Wooden, our coach, is a legend. But you know that …"

The Student Union. The Library. Bruin Walk. The original campus buildings with their iconic architecture, featured in an endless list of movies. Nick wanted to see Jackie Robinson Field, but that would have to wait. They ended the tour at Donna's dorm building and the spartan room she shared, barely space for two beds and two desks. It was clear she'd fallen in love with the place. Nick had to admit the campus was beautiful, modern, crowded, exciting. He was happy for her.

They left the campus and headed for Westwood Village, Donna once again pointing out the landmarks. They settled on a sandwich shop for lunch and then retrieved Nick's car for a drive to Santa Monica and the beach. He put the top down and they donned sunglasses, pretending to be celebrities while the radio blared Simon and Garfunkel's "Cecilia."

The Santa Monica Pier was crowded, interesting, odd, an eclectic mix of people from every strata of society. For Nick, some of the area was stunning and beautiful, but much of it seemed broken down and grubby. Looking into the distance, the air was brown and the buildings seemed to shimmer in the smog. He'd take Northern California over L.A., hands down.

Later that evening, they found a café on Beverly Drive for dinner. They ordered wine, showed their fake IDs, and kept straight faces as the waiter stared at them in disbelief. From there it was on to the movies to see *Five Easy Pieces*, a new release generating a lot of buzz. They weren't disappointed.

It had been a full day, with more to follow on Sunday. Nick was exhausted when they arrived at the room he'd rented at a Travelodge on Santa Monica Boulevard. Still, he was glad to finally be alone with Donna. He pulled her close and kissed her.

"Don't …" Donna said.

"What's wrong?"

"We can't make love, Nick."

"What? Why?"

"I stopped taking the pill."

"I can go to a drug store …"

"No. I don't trust those things." She snuggled her head against his chest.

"Geez, Donna, why did you …?"

"Just hold me, okay?"

Nick wasn't surprised. He'd sensed something all day, despite the fun—a distance, a pulling away. Donna was moving on, exploring her independence. He wondered how long it would be before she gave him the speech. *This long-distance thing just doesn't work, Nick. I really think we should see other people. I'll always care for you. God, you were my first, but blah, blah, blah …* It was just a matter of time.

It was the first and only time they would spend an entire night together. Donna slept soundly.

Nick left Sunday afternoon, bracing for the long drive home. He'd done his best to stay upbeat and not pout, to avoid playing the disappointed lover. Heading up the Grapevine, he wasn't sure he'd pulled it off.

Just before he reached Gorman, steam began to pour from under the hood of the car. Nick exited the freeway and rolled into a service station. It was a blown radiator hose, an easy fix, but the repair bays were full, only one mechanic on duty, other cars and their angry drivers ahead of him. Nothing to do but wait. He found a payphone and called home to let his mom know he'd be delayed. She would call Gus and let him know Nick might not be in on Monday.

Sleeping in a 1946 Ford Coupe was not easy for a guy who stood six two. Nick did his best, a jacket rolled up to act as a pillow. He jolted awake several times during the night, a sharp pain in his neck, as trucks roared by on the freeway.

It was the cherry on this weekend sundae. Or rather, another turd in the punch bowl.

13

The paving crew assembled at the side of Glen Cove Road on a clear October morning, waiting for the truck that hauled the compressor to arrive. They talked, laughed, smoked, drank coffee from red thermos cups, and enjoyed the early morning sunlight.

Nick looked to the east, the sun in his eyes, toward the old Victorian mansion set well back from the main road. The well-maintained two-story was the home of the Glen Cove brothel, an institution in the Vallejo area. It had been in business for as long as Nick could remember, out in the rolling hills surrounded by grazing land.

"Is this place even in the city limits?" He posed the question to Joe Jacoby, their veteran foreman.

"Hell, I don't know. If it's not technically, then it's an honorary annex." The men surrounding Joe had a good laugh.

STREET CRED

The assignment this Monday morning was to repair the long access drive that led from Glen Cove Road to the parking lot that fronted the mansion. Joe had sprayed white paint to mark several sections that required repair. They would break out the old asphalt with a jackhammer, haul the debris away, and do their expert job of preparing the base, spreading the new paving material, raking and rolling.

Joe had a story to share. "So, Paddy walks into his local pub. He's got this great big lump and a bruise on his forehead. Bartender says, 'Saints preserve us, Paddy. Wot happened to you?' Paddy says, 'Aye, Michael, me friend, I had a fight wit me girl. I called her a two-bit whore.' Michael says, 'Aye lad, what then?' Paddy says, 'She hit me wit a bag of quarters.'"

The men threw back their heads and laughed. One spit coffee through his nose. They'd heard it before, but nobody told a joke like Joe. For his part, Joe was thinking ahead to his next story when a white panel truck crested the hill from the north, heading their way. As it grew near, they saw the blue lettering on the side: Louisiana Steam Laundry, a respected business that had been around since the war years, a legendary sponsor of youth sports in town. Behind the wheel of the truck, Nick recognized his friend and former teammate, Jim Coolidge. Jim stopped where the crew was gathered and rolled down the window.

"Hi, guys. Hey, Nick! What are you doin' here?" Jim smiled and set the brake on the old truck.

"Hi, Jimmy. I should ask you the same question." Nick approached the truck and clapped a hand on Jim's shoulder. "I'm working for the Street Department. We're gonna patch the driveway here."

"You're paving the whorehouse? Damn, that's some job." He looked down the long access road where Joe's spray paint was in evidence.

"How 'bout you, Jim?"

"I deliver clean sheets and towels, pick up the dirty laundry. Twice a week."

"You're kidding!" Nick stared at his friend. Was this a put-on?

"Nope, dead serious. They're a good account. Pay their bills right on time. The places I used to deliver to, down on Lower Georgia, it was cash only. No cash, no laundry."

Nick couldn't believe it. "Wait a minute. You used to deliver on Lower Georgia too?"

"Sure did. Several places."

Nick nodded toward the old mansion. "What's it like in there?" He couldn't help but smile. What a great job, delivering laundry to Glen Cove.

"Oh, I go to the back door, into the kitchen. Looks like any other kitchen."

Nick was dying to ask. "Ever meet any of the girls?"

"Yeah, a few. They're in the kitchen sometimes, having coffee or fixing breakfast."

"No shit? What are they like?"

"Hate to disappoint you, Nick, but sittin' around—jeans and sweatshirts, no makeup, no fancy dresses—they're just people. Some are prettier than others, but just people." Jim was serious now, quiet and reflective.

Nick had one last question. "You ever get an offer in there?"

Jim released the brake and threw the truck into gear as Nick stepped back. "Ha! What do you think?" He waved, let out the clutch, and rolled away, turning onto the long, rutted, about-to-be-patched road. "See ya later, buddy."

Nick turned to see the compressor rig approaching from the north. Jim had arrived just in time to make his delivery and pickup. It was time to go to work repairing the cathouse drive.

"I don't know, Sis. I'm not sure this makes sense."

Nick's sister, Ella, didn't want to hear it. "Why? What doesn't make sense? Virginia is a great university. You've got the grades, you've got the SATs, you've submitted your transcript and they'll accept your JC credits. What's the problem?"

"Money, Ella. Dollars and cents. Out-of-state tuition is high. Baseball scholarships are partial and may not even cover tuition. Not to mention fees, books, room and board."

"Hey, you'll never know until you go see for yourself, see the campus, meet some of the guys, see what they are offering. Just go and enjoy the journey."

They sat at the table in Ella's kitchen in Daly City, a cool wind blowing up the breezeway and through the open window. Ella would drop Nick off at San Francisco International on Friday morning for the nonstop jet to Washington, DC. There he'd connect with a local carrier for the short flight into Charlottesville.

Nick would spend the weekend on the University of Virginia campus and return to San Francisco on Sunday, hopefully with a scholarship offer in hand.

"What about Mom?" Again, Nick worried about money.

"Mom will be fine." Ella reached across the table to squeeze his hand. "She has Dad's pension. She has healthcare through his Navy benefits. And Les and I can help if she needs it." She tightened her grip. "Look, baby brother, you have a chance to be the first in our family to graduate from college. Now go and do it. Okay?"

Nick looked out the kitchen window as the sun dipped below the hills to the west, the sky a deep shade of orange. Was it money he was worried about or the thought of leaving home—the only home he'd ever known? Virginia seemed a world away.

Assistant Coach Charles "Chip" Murphy met Nick at the Charlottesville airport. They retrieved Nick's bag, found Chip's car in the parking lot, and headed for the university campus. Coach Murphy sketched out a plan for the weekend.

"We'll take a quick ride around the campus and then stop off at the office so you can meet Coach West. Good man, you'll like him. Then I'll take you over, show you the ballyard and our training facilities."

Murphy's accent was from south of the Mason-Dixon Line, like honey on a Georgia peach. The tension in Nick's shoulders began to ease.

"How ya feelin', son? I know it's a long flight. You okay?"

"I'm fine, Coach. Thanks."

"Later, I'll drop you off where you'll be stayin'. It's a house over on Fourteenth Street, where several of the guys rent. I think there are about four of 'em in there. We call it the Baseball House." Chip laughed. "Anyway, they're gonna take you in for the weekend."

They drove on, turning onto University Drive, Coach Murphy pointing out the landmarks as they passed. Nick was fascinated. History was his favorite subject, and Thomas Jefferson had always been a person of great interest. And here was Nicholas Shane Jr., touring Mr. Jefferson's university. He couldn't wait to see the classic Rotunda and what Jefferson referred to as his Academic Village— residence units that flanked the Lawn, a terraced expanse of grass where graduating classes assemble every spring to receive their diplomas.

For Nick, only Washington, Lincoln, and FDR stood out in the history of the country like Jefferson. "We hold these truths to be self-evident, that all men are created equal …" God, what a revolutionary idea! A phrase that sparked movements and wound up in constitutions all around the world, yet written by a man who owned slaves until the day he died. It was the power of the words, the genie let out of the bottle, the bullet that could never be unfired.

Nick wondered whether there would be time to travel out to Monticello, Jefferson's home, where he and Captain Merriweather Lewis planned the Corps of Discovery Expedition, sending Lewis and Lt. William Clark off to explore the Louisiana Purchase.

They approached the Rotunda, the architectural icon of the campus. At the top of the steps rising from the avenue, the statue of Jefferson stood gazing off into the distance. What an enigma, this man who designed his home to keep the household slaves out of sight—and yet fathered children with Sally Hemmings, one of the slaves he sought to hide. Nick was engulfed by the sense of history.

"Coach, aren't the Serpentine Walls around here, in this area?

Chip Murphy laughed. "Well, I'll be damned. You've done your homework, son. Let me find a place to park. We'll take a walk around."

Coach Murphy dropped Nick off at the Baseball House and introduced him to the young men who would be his hosts for the weekend. The old home was an odd structure. A covered porch ran the length of the front of the house, and from the street it looked like a single story. But the lot sloped down in the back to a gully choked with wild vines and overgrown shrubs. From the back of the lot, the lower level of the structure was visible. There were three bedrooms on the main floor, along with a large living room, a full bath, and spacious kitchen. The lower floor had two rooms, one large and one very small, plus a jerry-rigged toilet and shower.

Chip Murphy left Nick with a word of caution. "Watch out for these guys. I hope you like to party." They all laughed, except for Coach Murphy.

Nick did his best to remember names as his four hosts introduced themselves. There was Dan, short and stocky with bulging forearms, who seemed to take charge right away. Matt was tall and lean with a shock of unruly black hair. Paul had a great smile and a firm handshake. And Tyler, his cap spun around backwards, had a mischievous grin on his handsome face. Nick guessed their positions: catcher, pitcher, outfield, second base. He was close.

"Hey, you picked a great weekend, man." Nick liked the way Dan held eye contact. "Tomorrow night is Halloween. We're having a party here. We'll have to get you some kind of costume."

Nick laughed. "I came prepared, like a good Boy Scout."

"What? You brought a costume?"

"Yeah. I figured there'd be something going on for Halloween."

"So, what's your costume, man?" They looked at Nick in anticipation.

"I've got a Mets cap and jersey with McGraw on the back. And a left-handed glove. Oh, and some eye-black, too." Nick smiled and waited for it to sink in.

"Ah, cool, man! You're going as Tug McGraw. Where'd you get that idea?"

"Tug's from my hometown. Vallejo, California. He played at the same junior college as me, only about six years ago, 1963–64." Nick was pleased that his costume plan went over well.

Dan took charge again. "Come on, I'll give you a tour of the house. This is the kitchen. I'm gonna grab a beer. You want one?" Nick accepted the cold can and followed Dan into the living room. "We'll probably go out tonight, meet some of the guys at a joint up on The Corner—that's over on University, just a couple of blocks. You okay with that?"

"Sure. I brought my ID. Says I'm twenty-five. Do I look it?" Nick laughed.

"Damn! You *are* prepared. Hey, this is gonna be great."

Nick followed Dan through the upper floor and then down to the lower level. *I like these guys. Decent house too. Close to the campus. I wonder if they have an empty room here? Whoa, slow down, buddy boy. Cart before the horse.*

15

The house filled up with guys and dolls in various costumes. To Nick, they were all strangers in disguise. Pumpkins lined the walk that led to the porch, carved in grotesque expressions; candles flickered inside to cast a strange orange glow. Two washtubs were prominent in the kitchen, filled with aluminum cans of beer floating in a sea of ice. Furniture in the front room had been pushed aside to clear the ancient hardwood floor for dancing. A Beatles album was playing as several couples moved to the music. This would be a fine Halloween party if the police stayed away.

Dan took Nick through the crowd, introducing him to members of the baseball team who would be returning for the coming season. To a man, they seemed fascinated by a visitor from California, the Golden State, land of fruits, nuts, and movie stars. They laughed at his costume, though a few had to be reminded. "Who, exactly, is McGraw? Oh, yeah—Tug and the 1969 Mets. Ha!"

There was a girl wearing a Wonder Woman costume. He couldn't stop glancing her way. Or was he staring? Long black hair. Very dark eyes. Amazing cheekbones. Gleaming white teeth. Tall and lean, like a distance runner. She caught him looking again and walked toward him with a beautiful smile.

"Hi. I'm Kellen."

The noise was deafening. "Ellen?"

She leaned close to his ear. "Kellen."

"Oh, hi. I'm Nick."

"Are you the recruit from California?"

"Yeah. How could you tell?" Nick laughed.

"You don't look like you're from around here. Most guys don't wear shorts and flip-flops this time of year. Why UVA? How did that happen?"

"I know a guy who knows a guy." Dante Benedetti's face flashed in Nick's mind.

"What?" Her smile was dazzling. Nick didn't know teeth could be that white.

"Just kidding. I need a place to play baseball in exchange for a degree. Did I come to the right place?"

Kellen motioned toward the front porch. "Let's go out front, get some air."

Out on the porch, the noise level dropped several decibels, and the conversation continued. Kellen was from Norfolk, a navy brat who'd lived on both coasts. She was entering her third year, majoring in political science, and thinking about law school. Nick talked about his goal of becoming a teacher with a focus on history, and maybe coaching on the side. He liked what he'd seen in Charlottesville—beautiful campus, great guys. He hoped to leave with a scholarship offer.

"Dan tells me you're a good guy. I'm sure that's what he'll tell the coaches."

"You think so? I'm meeting with Coach Murphy and Coach West tomorrow for breakfast, before I go to the airport. I should find out then." Nick couldn't hide the doubt in his voice.

"Hey, just relax and have fun. They don't bring guys across the country if they're not serious."

Nick looked away. "Even if I get an offer, it's gonna be tough. I'll be lucky if it covers tuition. I'll need to find a job, doing something."

"Ever tend bar, Nick?"

"What? No. But I'm a quick study."

"How old are you?"

"Twenty now. I'll be twenty-one in May. Why?" Nick was curious. Where was this leading?

"I tend bar part-time at O'Neil's. It's a dive up on The Corner. I could introduce you to my boss." The brilliant smile was back. Nick couldn't believe his luck.

He was aware of a commotion behind him. He turned to see a very large, angry young man moving toward him. Dan had a hand on the man's arm, trying to restrain him.

"Are you having fun here, Hollywood?" He moved within inches of Nick's face.

"Yeah, pretty much." Nick tried to smile. "Hi, I'm Nick. Don't think we've met."

"Oh, so fuckin' polite! Well, Nick, this girl you're chattin' up is *my* girl. *Capiche?*"

"Hey, sorry, man. I didn't know." Nick raised his hands, a hands-off gesture.

Kellen stepped forward and pushed hard on the man's chest, knocking him back several feet. "Shut the fuck up, Billy! I'll talk to anyone I want. You do not own me!"

Several guys surrounded Billy and led him away, mumbling and cursing. Kellen turned back to Nick.

"Ignore him. He can be such a dick sometimes. Hey, good luck tomorrow. And if you want that introduction, let me know. Dan has my number." She turned and walked away into the crowd.

Nick stayed on the porch for a while, until his heart stopped racing.

The Waffle House was crowded, a typical Sunday morning. They waited for a booth in the nonsmoking section, though the entire restaurant was under a cloud of smoke. Without a doubt, Virginia was tobacco country.

Nick took a seat across from the two coaches. The conversation consisted of small talk regarding Nick's weekend. How did he like the campus? Did the guys show him the field, the training facility, the lockers over at University Hall? Did he get to see much of Charlottesville? Their waitress came to clear away the breakfast dishes and pour more coffee. Coach Jim West was a stocky man with a round face, wire-rimmed glasses, and curly brown hair. He took control of the conversation.

"Nick, we've heard good things from the guys at the Baseball House. Sounds like you fit right in."

"They're great guys, sir. I had a lot of fun."

"Y'know, we've talked to Coach McWilliams at Vallejo JC, and to Dante Benedetti in San Francisco. They have good things to say about you. We have great respect for both of those men." Nick nodded in agreement. His pulse thumped at his temples. Coach West continued. "They both agree on one thing. You seem to play every game with a smile on your face. Tell us about that, son. What's that all about?"

Nick felt the heat rising on his neck. He looked at the men across the table, from one to the other. How could he answer that question? How do you explain the feeling when you run onto a baseball diamond and believe you can fly? Or how it feels when you time your dive perfectly and the ball sticks in your glove for the out? Or what it's like when you rip a line drive, on the absolute sweet spot of the bat, and it's so perfect you don't even feel it in your hands? Or being part of a real team, competing against the best, winning or losing, celebrating or crying, just a bunch of guys who become one, forever. He couldn't find the words, not if he sat there for a week. But he had to say something.

"It's just … I mean, the game … it's a blessing, Coach. You *have* to smile." Nick was embarrassed now. Had he blown it? Made a fool of himself?

The two men across from Nick were quiet. The silence stretched to the point of being awkward. Coach West looked at his assistant and nodded. He cleared his throat and turned back to Nick.

"Son, we want you to play for us, to be a Cavalier, bring some of that love to Virginia." West opened a manila folder. "This is an offer letter. You'd enter as a third year, fall semester '71. I wish it could be more, but it should cover your tuition. Take this home and talk to your family. If you decide to accept, we'll need your letter of intent by November 11." He moved the folder across the table toward Nick, then smiled and extended his hand. Nick shook it firmly.

They chatted a while longer, the coaches sketching out their plans for the coming season, their hopes of making the NCAA postseason tournament for the first time in the history of the program. Looking ahead, they made no promises, only that Nick would have a chance to compete for a position in the outfield. If he accepted.

Nick's head was spinning as they left the Waffle House and headed for the airport.

16

ick sat at a long wooden table and finished his lunch, aware of the conversations around him but paying little attention. Near the wall on the south side of the building, a group was involved in pitching quarters: closest to the wall kept 'em all. Joe Jacoby was cleaning up, winning almost every toss and maintaining a steady stream of comments designed to keep the suckers pitching. At another table, a four-handed game of casino was underway at full volume. The stakes were modest, the passions high.

The Street Department had taken over this warehouse, situated near the waterfront, sometime in the late fifties. The former owner, Levi Strauss, had used it to store raw material. It provided a warm, dry place for the crew to get in out of the weather, eat lunch, play cards, and kill time before hitting the bricks. Work on the streets was slow during late fall and winter, especially when the rains came. Major repair projects were on hold. The typical assignments were patching potholes or working with the Parks Department to prune the bare trees that lined neighborhood streets.

It was the day before Thanksgiving, and the men were looking forward to a long weekend. Thursday and Friday were paid holidays, one of the perks afforded city workers. Nick would spend the holiday weekend in San Francisco with his mom, sister, and brother-in-law. Good food, good wine, lively debates around the dinner table. He had hoped to spend it with Donna, but she'd opted at the last minute to stay in L.A., citing work on a class project that was due. It seemed the distance between them was growing like a foreign weed.

Gus Cordeiro slid onto the bench across the table from Nick.

"So, Joe College, how's it goin'? Fill me in on the latest."

Nick laughed. He hadn't heard the nickname in a while. "I think it's coming together, Gus. I signed the letter of intent early this month, right after I got back from Charlottesville. I start school in August of next year. Turns out the guys at the house where I stayed back there have an empty room. The rent is really cheap, mainly because it's like a cell in the basement, barely big enough for a bed and desk. And I met somebody who can possibly hook me up with a part-time job tending bar."

"What?" Gus laughed out loud. "You don't know anything about tending bar."

"No big deal. I've got a book, and I'll do my homework. Besides, it's a college town. How hard is it to open a bottle of beer?" Nick was serious. He'd already borrowed a book from a friend: *The Bartenders Guide—Pour Your Path to Success.*

"What do you think of the coaches?"

"I like 'em. And they say the guys that will be back for the '72 season are a good group. They think they'll be competitive in the ACC, maybe get a bid for the NCAA tournament. That would be a first for the program. I don't know, Gus, it all looks good."

"Good for you, Nick. Just stick with the plan. I want you gone come August of '71. Got it?" Gus looked around at his crew while Joe Jacoby collected another pocketful of quarters. "You're gonna be working with the guys on the pier this afternoon. The weather is breaking up. We can get a good start on the job."

"Question, Gus. Why are we working on the Ryder Street pier? Is that Street Department stuff?"

"It's a contract thing, kid. Besides, they're thinking about running the car ferries again, Ryder Street to the shipyard, so the pier is an extension of the street." Gus got up and called for attention. "Okay, guys. Break's over. Let's get back out there."

The men wrapped up their fun and games, gathered their lunch pails, and headed for the door. Nick hadn't been to Ryder Street in years. The old pier, built during the World War II boom, ended in a slip where car ferries could dock to unload and load vehicles. Nick and his friends fished there when they were kids.

It was 4:00 p.m., the sun beginning to sink in the west. It would be dark by 5:15 or thereabouts. The afternoon task had been to rip out and replace cross beam supports under the pier. Old, rotted timbers floated in the shallow water while new beams, heavy with creosote, were bolted into place. To aid this task, two flat-bottom skiffs had been rented from the Lemon Street Resort, just up the channel from Ryder Street.

Nick's job was simple. He was stationed in one of the skiffs, holding it close to a massive piling, passing the necessary tools to the men working under the pier. Old Mike Bouchka sat in the second skiff about ten feet away, wrapped in a heavy jacket, a black watch cap pulled down over his ears. He was sound asleep.

Nick heard laughter from the deck of the pier, eight feet above. He looked up to see Norm Runyon and several other men looking down at Mike and laughing. He heard Norm say, "Watch this." Runyon leaned over the railing holding an eight-pound sledgehammer in his right hand. The hammer would hit the deck of the skiff with a bang and give Mike a good scare. A little harmless fun with the old man. Norm released the hammer and Nick watched in shock as it crashed through the rotted hull of the old boat and disappeared.

Norm got the reaction he was looking for. Mike jolted awake and hollered, "You rotten sonofabitch!" They all watched, frozen, as water rushed through the hole left by the hammer, the skiff sinking in the muddy Mare Island Strait with Mike aboard.

Nick pushed off the piling, sliding his skiff toward Mike's. He grabbed an oar and jammed it into the shallow water against the muddy bottom, leaning hard until the boats came together. Mike was attempting to stand, the water up to his shins. Nick reached out and grabbed Mike's jacket with both hands and pulled him—stumbling, falling—into Nick's skiff. For a few seconds, they were face-to-face, the smell of coffee and onions on Mike's breath, a look of fear and bewilderment in his eyes. Nick struggled to get the old man seated and secure. Then he had the overwhelming urge to punch Norm Runyon in the mouth. He wasn't alone. Voices were raised all over the pier.

"Goddamn it, Norm!"

"Are you nuts?"

"You trying to kill the old guy?"

It came like thunder from the west end of the pier. Gus Cordeiro had been with a group working on the ferry slip. Now he was running toward Norm Runyon, raging at the top of his lungs. All voices fell silent, in awe of Gus's fury.

"Runyon! God damn it! What in the hell were you thinking? Use your frickin' head! For God's sake, man! You're damn lucky the water is shallow there ..."

The tirade went on and on. Nick had never seen Gus so angry. He felt sorry for Norm Runyon, but only for a moment. Norm stood with his head down, hat in hand, mumbling apologies. He had it coming.

Nick rowed the skiff toward the shore, thirty yards away. Several guys came down the bank to help secure the boat and get Mike safely to dry land.

Meanwhile, Gus had regained composure. He directed his men to secure the worksite for the day and then took Mike by the arm, leading him toward a truck parked out on Ryder Street. He would drive Mike home.

Gus's explosion would become part of department lore, growing louder and longer with each retelling. They would all learn to laugh at Norm's prank gone bad, but it would take a long time.

17

Nick and Donna sat on the steps outside Morgan's apartment, away for the moment from the New Year's Eve party. The crowd inside swung between raucous laughter and the steady buzz of conversation. The December night air felt good, refreshing. Donna wrapped her coat tightly about her against the chill. She'd be leaving soon to return to Los Angeles, ready to begin a new semester at UCLA. Nick shared his news about Virginia. They paused to listen to the commotion from within the apartment.

"Nick, I'm glad we got to spend time together while I've been home. It really was a wonderful Christmas."

"Yeah, it was. Good times with your family. And mine." He took her hand in his. "I'm happy for you, Donna, that it's going so well for you. If anybody deserves it, it's you."

She was quiet for a moment. When she spoke, there was a thickness in her voice. "Look, Nick, I know it's been hard for you. I mean, we're not a couple like we were before, and I know that's sad for you. For me too. But it's the right thing, for both of us." She looked at him, pleading her case.

It was another dagger to Nick's heart. Donna was moving on, trying to let him down easy, to soften the blow. The pain got to him and stirred a little anger. His words came without much thought, dripping with sarcasm.

"Donna, this long-distance thing isn't working for either of us. I really think we should see other people. I'll always care for you. My God, you were my first ..." His voice broke and he couldn't continue.

The words stung. "Don't be mean, Nick. That's not like you. Don't make what we had cheap. I loved you, and I know you loved me. Can't we keep that?"

All Nick heard was *loved*. Past tense.

A loud *pop* sounded inside the apartment as a champagne cork flew. Zeke's voice rose above the noise. "Come on, everybody. Fill your glasses."

Nick stood up. "Should we go back in? It's almost midnight."

Donna stood next to him, just as the countdown began.

"Five ... four ... three ... two ... one. Happy New Year!"

"Auld Lang Syne" blared from the television set inside, and the party sang along.

Donna threw her arms around Nick's neck and kissed him long and deep with a passion he hadn't felt in months. When she stepped back, her eyes were filled with tears. She took his hand and led him up the stairs, back to the party.

18

The parking lot at Scotty's was nearly empty on this midweek evening in January. Through the plate glass windows of the cafe, Nick saw a handful of customers enjoying the best coffee and doughnuts in town. Grady sat at the far end of the counter on the left side. The bell above the front door rang brightly as Nick entered and made his way to the stool next to his friend.

"Hey, buddy. How's it goin'?" The waitress approached and Nick ordered a glazed doughnut and a cup of coffee.

"It goes, Nickie, it goes. How's by you?"

They chatted for a while about life in general—work, the 49ers, the Warriors—and then Grady got to the point of their meeting.

"Your message said you had something for me, Nick. What's up?"

"I got a letter from Jeff, from Vietnam, addressed to both of us. I knew you'd want to read it." Nick pulled the envelope from the pocket of his jacket and handed it to Grady.

"Wow." Grady took a few seconds to turn the envelope in his hands, amazed at the cluster of stamps and the detailed return address. He removed the letter and unfolded it. A smile crossed his face as he recognized Jeff's neat handwriting. He glanced at Nick and then read silently.

> Dear Nick and Grady (one letter for two buddies—how efficient),
>
> Well, here I am, though I'm not supposed to say exactly where. I think this would be a beautiful country if we weren't blowing it up. Picture a rice paddy the size of several football fields, a lone figure in a broad straw hat plowing the field behind a water buffalo, great blue mountains in the background. Now picture the buffalo dead and bloated, feet in the air, the rice paddy pocked by bomb craters, that lone figure long gone.
>
> Hey, we're just doing our job. Right?
>
> Our job is called search and destroy, though it should be bait and switch. We go out on patrol, trying to find the VC or the ARVN. We get our asses caught in an ambush, and then we call in air strikes to blow the shit out of 'em. Our kill ratio is great. We get ten of them for every one of us. The problem is, I knew that one. We shared a tent, we shared rations this morning. I knew his parents' names, and he knew mine. Now he's in a pine box, heading home. Bait and switch.
>
> I don't know what they're telling you at home, but we've got a term over here that sums it up. FUBAR—Fucked Up Beyond All Recognition. If they send me home in a box, I want you to

promise to scatter my ashes at Timber Cove.
Pinky-swear, okay?

Take care, guys. Say a prayer for me.
Your buddy, Jeff

"Ah, shit, Nick. Holy freakin' shit." Grady dropped the letter on the counter and blinked back tears. "We should never have let him go. Not in a million years. We should have thrown him in your car and driven his ass to Canada."

"I know. I know, man. Look, all we can do is pray and hope for the best—"

"It should be me over there. You know that, don't you? I'm the one who was ready to go. Goddamn it, Nick. Just goddamn it."

The waitress started toward them, a full pot of coffee in hand, ready to refill their cups She read the situation and turned away. Now was not the time for more coffee.

19

Wind and rain whipped through the North Bay in February. Nick didn't mind. His new assignment had him working indoors for the time being.

Gus Cordeiro had taken on a new task for his crew, partnering with the Vallejo Fire Department on a weed abatement program. The plan was to spray open fields and vacant lots with a combination herbicide and sterilant and thereby eliminate potential grass fires in the dry months. A four-wheel-drive truck had been outfitted with a spray system. A large tank in the truck bed fed a spray bar mounted on the front bumper. The spray bar covered a path fifteen feet wide over open ground; it folded in for travel on the streets. A hose-and-nozzle attachment provided for places the bar couldn't reach.

Through January and February, Nick and his partner worked with the VFD captain in charge of the project, preparing plat maps that marked the lots and fields to be sprayed. It was good to be warm and dry, working upstairs in Station 21 on Marin Street.

But it was too good to last. The plan was to begin spraying as soon as the rains subsided, likely to be early in March.

Marty Nyland was Nick's partner. A shade under six feet tall, Marty was built like a two-hundred-pound block of granite. In his early thirties now, he'd been the youngest man in the Street Department until Nick came along. Marty could charm with a smile, the twinkle in his eye, and the sense that he was always up to some mischief. Nick liked him immediately.

"Okay, guys. That's enough for today." Captain Ferris patted Nick on the back. "We'll pick up from here tomorrow. We're almost done with the maps."

Nick and Marty closed the map books, stored their marking pens, and headed downstairs.

"Hey, Nick. I've gotta make a couple of quick stops on the way home. Okay?"

"Sure. No problem, Marty." Nick's old Ford was being serviced, and Marty had given him a ride to work. "Where are we going?"

"My girlfriend left her wallet at home. I'm gonna pick it up and take it to her at work. The house isn't far from here."

"Where does she work?"

Marty smiled. "Remember the bar on Sonoma Boulevard called Shorty's?"

"Yeah. Topless place, right?"

"Yeah, well, now it's bottomless. Shorty changed the name to Bottoms Up. She works there."

"Oh … what does she do? Waitress? Tend bar?"

"No. She's a dancer."

Nick let that answer hang in the air. He turned to look at his partner, trying to judge the grin on Marty's face.

Nick followed Marty into Bottoms Up and stood near the door, waiting for his eyes to adjust to the dim light. It didn't take long. The stage for the dancers was built above and behind the back bar, and it was well-lit. The club was crowded with guys stopping after work to drink and gawk at the nude dancers. Nick looked up to the stage and his jaw dropped. The girl on stage, a beautiful brunette wearing black stilettos, danced sensuously around a bent-wood chair, using a heart-shaped pillow as a prop. He'd never seen a woman so perfect. Could she be real? Was she a hologram? He felt a hard slap on his arm and turned to see Marty glaring at him.

"You're drooling, man. Cool your jets." Marty smiled. Or was it a sneer?

Nick mumbled something in response and turned back to the stage as the song ended. The crowd erupted in applause as the dancer took a quick bow and then slipped on a shirt that had been draped over the chair. She bowed again, picked up a pair of black panties from the chair, and exited to the rear of the stage. Marty gripped Nick's elbow and led him to the bar. They took stools vacated by customers now heading for the door. Marty signaled the bartender and two bottles of beer quickly appeared.

"Hi, sweetie. Did you bring my wallet?"

Nick turned to see the girl who'd just left the stage. She reached up to plant a quick kiss on Marty's lips.

"Yeah, babe. Here ya go." Marty handed the wallet to her. "Sibley, this is my partner Nick. Nick, this is my girl, Sibley."

Nick got up from the stool quickly. "Hi, Sibley. Nicetomeetya." His tongue felt fat, words ran together. He motioned for the girl to take his stool.

"Thank you, kind sir." She was even prettier up close than on stage. "Marty, would you get me a 7 Up, sweetie?" She turned to Nick. "I'm new here. Just started this week. I'm still trying to get my routine worked out."

She smiled and Nick felt his knees wobble. If she was fishing for a compliment, Nick was hooked. "Oh, you were great." His cheeks flushed. "I mean *really* great."

She wore a dark blue men's shirt with a button-down collar, and it flashed through Nick's mind that she was naked under that neatly pressed garment. He reached for his beer and nearly knocked the bottle over. Marty and Sibley laughed.

They chatted for a while, finished their drinks, and said goodbye to Sibley. She headed for a back room to get ready for her next set while Nick and Marty made their way to the door.

"So, what do you think, buddy?" Marty grinned at Nick as they came to the car.

Nick looked at Marty with new appreciation. "Wow!" he said. It was the only word that fit.

20

Nick had turned the one-car garage into a gym. His mom didn't mind. Her gray Chevy Nova sat in the driveway, Nick's old Ford convertible at the curb in front of the house. A weight bench, barbells, and various free weights were stacked and racked around the cement floor of the garage. A bright blue two-inch thick mat provided for floor exercises.

Work every quadrant, top to bottom. Add weight. Add reps. Feel the burn, that good sweet burn.

There was one device not seen in other gyms. A heavy cord hung from a metal eyelet screwed into the ceiling. The cord ended in a large knot, the knot positioned about waist high.

Nick grabbed the weighted bat he'd made, took his stance in an imaginary batter's box, swung the bat, and hit the knot at the end of the cord. The knot flew up, slapped the ceiling, and then returned to its original position. Nick took his stance and swung again. *Click* went the bat against the knot. *Whap* went the knot against the ceiling. *Click-whap*. Again and again.

Weight back, bat back, ready to stride. Quick hands. Quick wrists. Follow through. Balance, balance, balance all the way.

He'd added about eight ounces to the thirty-two-ounce bat by drilling holes in the barrel, melting lead fishing weights in a coffee can on a camp stove, and pouring the lead into the holes. He'd wrapped the barrel with white sports tape, and his training tool was ready. Fifty good hard swings, then fifty more. Take a breather, then two more sets of fifty. Another breather, then two more sets. Three hundred swings in total. This was Nick's regimen, and it worked because he believed in it, believed it developed his swing—added strength, added power, added distance.

Click-whap. Square it up. Click-whap. Love that sound!

It wasn't an original idea. Nick's dog-eared copy of *The Boys of Summer* sat on the desk in his bedroom, the chapter in which Roger Kahn visits George "Shotgun" Shuba flagged with a bookmark. Shuba used a forty-two-ounce bat and took six hundred swings a night, more than Nick could handle. But he was working on it, building up, adding reps.

You want five tools? You want power? Watch this, all you slackers!

Three hundred good, hard, balanced, competitive swings with a forty-ounce bat. Sweat poured from his body. When the weights and the swings were done, it was time to hit the streets for a run. Sweatpants, a sweatshirt, a rubberized warm-up jacket to protect against the cold and work up a good lather, and a towel tucked around his neck. Three, maybe three and a half miles. Every night accounted for. Workouts on even-numbered nights, recovery on the odds.

Gettin' stronger. Gettin' ready. Gettin' ready to play.

Nick talked to himself only when he worked out. Day in and day out, people took him for a quiet, soft-spoken guy. It was only here, in Mom's garage and out on a run, that he went a little crazy.

Best shape of my life. I'm ready. Are you ready for Nick Shane?

21

Weed abatement duty was no picnic. It was wet, cold, nasty work. Wet and cold because of the March weather, nasty because Nick had his suspicions about the stuff they were spraying on vacant lots and fields. Was it hazardous to your health?

Nick and Marty soldiered on, out in the weather except for the days when rain drove them inside. They wore long johns under their jeans, with several layers above the belt that could be peeled away if the sun came out. They'd been issued rubber boots that covered their pant legs up to the knee, as well as rubber gloves to prevent contact with the herbicide. The material needed extended contact with the emerging grass and weeds, at least a day or so, or the rain could wash it away and their work would be wasted. But the rains relented in March, with most storms staying well to the north, and so they plunged on with their routine. Fill the tank with water from a fire hydrant. Dump in the required sacks of the powdered weed killer. Activate the paddle mechanism in the tank that kept the mixture stirred. Consult their book of maps for the next area to be sprayed. And repeat again and again.

It was Friday, and not a moment too soon. Nick was ready for the weekend. They parked the spray rig in the corporation yard, changed out of their wet clothes in the locker shed, and headed for the parking lot. The tables were reversed tonight: Nick was giving Marty a ride home.

"Nick, can we swing by Sibley's place? I want to check on something. Only take a minute."

"Sure. No problem."

Nick turned left off Georgia Street and into Sibley's neighborhood. As they approached the house she shared with a roommate, Nick felt Marty tense beside him.

"Sonofabitch! That goddamn—"

Nick turned to Marty. "What? What's the problem?"

"See that Cadillac parked at the curb? That's the problem."

A late-model Caddy sedan, its black paint polished to a high gloss, sat in front of Sibley's house.

Marty laughed. "She's forgetting something—I still have the key." He dangled a house key for Nick to acknowledge.

Marty was out of the car and running for the front door before Nick came to a full stop. He shut off the engine, rolled down the window, and leaned back in the seat, too tired to care about Marty's troubles, whatever they might be. He closed his eyes and relaxed. His eyelids felt heavy.

Sibley's front door flew open and a man ran out onto the front porch, buck naked, struggling to get into a pair of white underpants. He managed to get both feet into the tighty-whities and pulled them up to cover his privates. He ran for the Cadillac but found the door locked.

STREET CRED

Marty appeared at the front door, his arms overflowing with clothes—what looked like a suit, shirt, sox, and shoes. The guy in the undies took off on a dead run down the sidewalk, turned right at the corner, and disappeared. Marty shook the suit jacket and then the pants, letting the contents spill out onto the lawn. He picked up a wallet and threw it onto the roof of the house, followed by a set of keys, and a pair of brown oxfords, first the left and then the right.

Sibley came out onto the porch wearing a short terrycloth robe tied at the waist. "You're a bastard, Marty!" Her voice rang down the street for all the neighbors to hear. "A real bastard. I'll date anybody I want. I'm calling the police. Hear that, Marty? The police!" She spun around and ran back into the house.

Marty opened the passenger door and jumped in. "Let's go, Nick. Our work here is done." His laughter echoed through the neighborhood.

Nick gunned the mighty V8, popped the clutch, and heard the wheels scream as he tore away from the curb. No need to wait around for the police to arrive. He started to ask, *So, how are things with Sibley?* But Marty was too busy laughing to listen.

22

Mike Bouchka's retirement party was set for early May. He'd made it to full-pension status thanks to Gus and the entire crew. Gus reserved the large meeting room at Terry's Restaurant out on Magazine Street, near the freeway. It would be a simple affair: a no-host cocktail hour, dinner, a few speakers, some parting gifts, then old Mike would be on his way. That was the plan.

Nick dressed in his best suit, happy to find it still fit. He thought about a tie but decided that was too formal. An open-collared, button-down shirt would fit the bill.

Cocktail hour was off to a rollicking start, bars set up on either side of the room, two bartenders busy at each station, mixing drinks and opening bottles. There was a sudden commotion at the door. Nick turned to see Marty enter with Sibley on his arm.

Surprise! They'd made up. Nick recalled the last time he'd seen Sibley, and he smiled.

The handsome couple made a grand entrance, though no one was looking at Marty. Sibley wore a form-fitting black cocktail dress, the hem cut just above the knee. The scooped neckline featured her exquisite cleavage. Her accessories included gold earrings and a necklace Cleopatra would have loved. This was a generous gift on Sibley's part because it allowed all the men to look down and say, "Oh my, what a lovely necklace." Not a man jack among them could recall the color of her eyes (a warm milk-chocolate with gold flecks).

It seemed the room had tipped and spilled all the men toward Sibley. Chaos threatened for a moment, and Nick was afraid Marty was going to have to punch a few noses. Then Dory Bouchka came to the rescue. She made her way through the crowd, greeted Sibley warmly, took her by the hand, and introduced her to old friends. Civility was restored.

Nick and Marty found a table and claimed three seats. Nick would sit on Sibley's left and Marty on her right, thus providing some protection from the guys coming by to admire her necklace.

The waitstaff began to file out of the kitchen, delivering salads to each table. The dinner choices were steak and baked potato, or baked chicken breast and mashed potatoes; steak for the red ticket holders, chicken for the blue. Large bottles of wine, both red and white, were delivered to each table, proudly displaying the Italian-Swiss Colony label, courtesy of an anonymous benefactor. It was all good, so long as you liked your steak medium or your chicken dry. As the dinner dishes were taken away and coffee cups refilled, the program got underway, Joe Jacoby acting as master of ceremonies. Joe had several new jokes to share, duly scrubbed so as not to offend sensitive ears. Thanks to cocktail hour and Italian-Swiss Colony's little old winemaker, the crowd was ready to laugh. Joe did not let them down.

At the head table with Mike and Dory, Nick was surprised to see Mayor Florence Douglas. That was quite an honor for Mike.

Madam Mayor made a few remarks, thanked Mike for his service to the country and the city, and then spent ten minutes extolling the wonderfulness of Vallejo. The director of public works (Nick missed his name in Joe's intro) came to the podium to present Mike with his retirement check. Short and sweet.

Gus rose to a rousing ovation—clapping, foot stomping, hoots and whistles. Again, short and sweet. Gus, as always, was a man of few words. He presented Mike with a gold shovel, like those used in groundbreaking ceremonies. Then there was the gift from the entire crew: round-trip tickets on United Airlines to Chicago so that Mike and Dory could visit Mike's mother. Nick shook his head in wonder. Mike's mom, now in her late eighties, was alive and well, living on the South Side.

Next it was time for the keynote. Joe introduced Dory Bouchka to a polite round of applause. A large screen was moved into place, and Dory proceeded to present a slide show, with photos dating back to Mike's childhood. No surprise to Nick, Dory was warm and funny and quite poignant at times. The chronology reached their wedding day, and there was Mike in his full-dress Navy uniform, a chief's stripes on his arm, and Dory beautiful in a lacy white gown. Nick saw the young Mike, ramrod straight and full of vigor, and a lump formed in his throat. Life could be cruel to the human body. Dory was nearing the end now, but there was one more slide for which Nick was not prepared. It flashed up on the screen, and he caught his breath.

"Nick Shane?" Dory looked around the room until she found him. "There you are. Nick, Mike tells me this is a picture of your dad."

Nick raised his hand and nodded to Dory. There in the photo were Mike and Nick's father, Mike clutching a pool cue and Dad holding a longneck bottle of Budweiser, both wearing their American Legion Post 104 caps and grinning at the camera. Nick smiled and blinked back tears.

Dory asked for the projector to be powered down. She had something to say, and she commanded their attention.

"There is something Mike and I need to tell all of you who worked with him through the years. We know what you did. We know the extra work you took on so that we can stand here today. We know it wasn't easy, or even fair to all of you. But we will never forget the kindness and love you've shown. From the bottom of our hearts, we say thank you, thank you, thank you."

Dory left the podium and returned to her seat, bathed in silence. Then slowly, a few at a time, people began to stand and clap their hands until everyone was standing. The ovation continued for several minutes.

The party wound down slowly. The bartenders had shut down as dinner was being served, and most of the wine had been dispatched. And yet folks lingered, reluctant to see the night end.

Nick said his goodbyes and made his way to the parking lot. A heavy case of the blues came over him. He thought about Donna. God, how he wished she was there beside him, holding his hand.

23

May 20 marked Nick's twenty-first birthday. He didn't feel like celebrating. The blues from the night of Mike's retirement party clung to him like flypaper. His mom insisted on some sort of observance, some recognition of the milestone, and so she planned a special dinner for the evening of Saturday, May 22. Ella, Nick's sister, would drive in from San Francisco, and Grady would stop by later in the evening to help blow out the candles.

Lucille Shane shopped at the commissary on the shipyard and brought home a lovely sirloin tip roast. She would whip up her much-admired mashed potatoes with pan gravy, along with a nice green salad. And of course, there'd be chocolate devil's food cake for dessert.

As they finished their cake and coffee, Grady insisted on taking Nick out for one quick drink, now that they were both of legal age and no longer needed their fake IDs. Grady practically ran to the car. He had something up his sleeve. He even held the door open for Nick, and then jumped behind the wheel and made a beeline for the 714 Club, a working-class saloon on Benicia Road near the freeway.

Nick nursed his drink at the bar while Grady excused himself to make a call from the pay phone in the back. He returned, took his stool, and grinned at Nick.

"Okay, buddy. I called the not-so-secret number and gave the not-so-secret password. The car from Glen Cove is on the way to pick us up. It's my treat in honor of your birthday."

"Ah, Grady, geez … I don't know, man." Nick hadn't anticipated this surprise.

"Come on, Nick. Can't back out now. The car is on the way." Grady couldn't suppress a laugh.

A few minutes later, Maisie, the gray-haired black woman who drove the pick-up car for the Glen Cove brothel, stuck her head in the door. Grady smiled and waved to catch her attention. The boys followed her to the car, an old Chevy sedan that was well-known around town. A favorite sport among high school kids was to follow Maisie on her rounds, honking their horns as she loaded customers into the vehicle. Thankfully, there were no followers tonight.

When they arrived at the old mansion out in the rolling hills, Nick tried to point out the sections along the drive where he and his workmates had performed repairs. But it was a moonless night; no way to admire the work.

They didn't have to wait long inside. Business was transacted quickly. Nick chose a girl with a nice smile and followed her up the stairs to a private room. It quickly became clear that his heart, among other things, wasn't into it.

"Mind if we just talk?" Nick was apologetic.

"Sure, honey. It's your dime." She flashed that nice smile again.

And talk they did—about life, love, work, plans for the future, favorite movies, books. It turns out the young lady was a fan of

Emily Dickinson. She recited two poems from memory—the one that begins, "There's a certain slant of light, / On winter afternoons …" and then her all-time favorite, "Ample make this bed / Make this bed with awe …" Her eyes were shining as she finished. Nick was touched by her love for the Belle of Amherst.

An hour later, as he made his way back down the stairs, he knew Grady would want a full accounting. Should he make up a good story? Nah. He decided on the plain, unvarnished truth. They were on their way back to the 714 Club, Maisie at the wheel, when Grady asked the question.

"Okay, Nick. Tell me about it. I want a blow-by-blow description."

"Sorry to disappoint you, pal. Nothing happened."

"What?" Grady was shocked. "What do you mean, nothing happened?"

"I mean nothing happened. The elevator was down." Nick heard Maisie laugh softly.

"Ah, man. No elevator?"

"Nope. Down in the basement. Couldn't even get to the first floor." Nick glanced at Maisie. Her shoulders were shaking.

"Wait a minute. Did she push all the buttons?" Grady wasn't buying Nick's story.

"Yep, but it was no use. A total power outage."

Grady mulled it over for a moment. "So … what did you do?"

"We talked. Turns out she's a big fan of Emily Dickinson. Recited a couple of poems for me."

"Oh, crap. So, I paid for a poetry recital in a cathouse?"

"Hey, don't feel bad, buddy. It was very nice. I had a great time."

It was quiet for a minute while Grady thought it over. "You know what? I think we have a song here. We'll call it 'The Elevator Blues.'"

Maisie burst out laughing, unable to contain herself. The three of them went to work putting together verses for the song. As they rolled down Benicia Road, the first verse came together with ease:

> Down in the basement with those elevator blues
> Got a power outage, don't know what to do
> Pushed all the buttons, but it ain't no use
> So, I'm stuck in the basement with those elevator
> blues …

There were more verses, some better than others. They pulled up in front of the 714 Club and finished in full-throated fortissimo:

> So, I'm stuck in the basement with those elevator
> bluuues!

It was a birthday Nick would never forget.

24

ick and Grady stood at the edge of the cliff, looking down on Timber Cove. It was a beautiful day, the sun high, the sky blue. Wind from the west picked up, as it did most days along the coast. Whitecaps dotted the open water beyond the cove.

"Where do you scatter ashes in a place like this?" Nick scanned the beach, weighing the possibilities.

"Don't look at me, buddy. No one ever asked until now."

"Maybe over there by the creek, where we pitched the tent last time?"

"Yeah, that would be good. Just mix the ashes into the sand." Grady made a tumbling gesture with his hands.

"Or how about around the point, on the rock where we always fish? That would be good."

"Yeah, but blowback could be a problem in this wind." Grady blinked, imagining the grit flying in the breeze.

"True. There's always the canyon. We could scatter some up there."

"Good idea. One of Jeff's favorite places."

"I say we scatter in all three spots. The beach, the rock, and the canyon. How 'bout that?"

"Okay." Grady turned to smile at Nick. "I love it when a plan comes together."

The car door slammed. Nick and Grady turned to see Jeff limping toward them, leaning hard on his cane. He'd been asleep in the back seat since they'd passed through Bodega Bay.

"What are you bozos up to?" Jeff stood next to Nick and surveyed the familiar scene.

"Not much," Nick replied. "Just deciding where we would have scattered your ashes."

"Oh, yeah?" Jeff brightened, anxious to hear the decision. "And where exactly would that be?"

Grady took charge in his best undertaker's voice. "On the beach by the creek. Around the point on the famous rock. And up the canyon, way back among the redwoods. I trust that's acceptable to the deceased?"

Jeff approved. "Hell, yeah! Three scatters for the old Jeffer. What's not to like?"

The three friends shared a laugh, and then Nick turned and walked to the car, pretending there was something important he needed to retrieve. He'd been convinced that Jeff would come home in that proverbial pine box, that they'd never again share the beauty of this beloved cove. The fact that they were there, together, overwhelmed Nick. He took the time to dry his eyes and clear his throat.

They made plans to help Jeff down the trail to the beach, his wounded leg still in recovery. They'd carry him piggyback if they had to. No camping or fishing planned for this trip, just a picnic feast in their favorite place on Earth. And they'd raise a few toasts to Jeff, one of the lucky ones who came home alive.

25

N ick flipped the pages on his desk calendar. The days crawled by. At last, June turned into July, and he officially became a "short timer" to all the guys in the department. Then it was July 30, his last day on the job.

The entire crew was gathered in the warehouse for Nick's farewell. After lunch, Gus made his way to the center of the large room and called for attention.

"Hey, listen up, guys. Your attention here." Gus waited for quiet. "Today is the last day for our man Nick Shane. Also known as Boots. Also known as Joe College." An outburst of laughter made Nick blush. "Nick is leaving us to begin his career as a scholarship athlete at the University of Virginia." Mock *ooh*s and *aah*s filled the room. "So, Nick, all the guys pitched in and got you a going-away present. Something I think you can use."

Joe Jacoby came from the back of the room carrying a large suitcase decorated with a bright blue bow.

Gus continued. "This Samsonite three-suiter is for you to use in your travels, Nick. 'Cause you're a guy who's going places."

This was a major speech for Gus Cordeiro, and it was met with applause and cries of "Way to go, Nick. Go get 'em, kid." Gus wasn't finished.

"There's one more thing, Nick. Something I think you'll like." Gus motioned with his hand and Dory Bouchka came forward out of the crowd, holding a small package wrapped in colorful paper. Mike shuffled over to join her.

Dory smiled. "Nick, Mike and I thought you might like to have this to hang on your wall or put on your desk." She handed the package to Nick. "Go ahead, honey. Open it."

Nick tore away the paper. Inside was a copy of the photo of Mike standing next to Nick's dad, an eight-by-ten print in a plain black frame. Nick was speechless. He hugged Dory and whispered, "Thank you," in her ear. He hugged Mike too, which was a little awkward and brought a round of laughter from the crew.

Gus closed the little ceremony. "Nick, you're fine young man." His voice thickened, the words coming with difficulty. "It's been great having you with us. We wish you the best. Now, go make us proud."

Norm Runyon piped up from a nearby table. "Hey, Nick, we got you a cake too." He lifted one side, tilting it for Nick to see. It was a large sheet cake with white frosting, decorated with a baseball diamond.

Joe Jacoby called out, "For God's sake, Norm, don't drop it!"

Nick went to Gus for one last hug. It had been a hell of a year.

There were last-minute errands to run, so Nick borrowed his mom's car. He'd sold his beloved '46 Ford convertible, though it broke his heart to do it. The cash would come in handy. He would leave the following day to fly east and begin his Virginia adventure. He cruised along Springs Road in his mom's gray '63 Chevy Nova sedan, a list of things to do resting on the seat next to him. Up ahead, a familiar sight came into focus. The white city paint truck was parked in the center of the street, thirty or more orange cones diverting traffic away to the right-hand lane. And there was Ralphie Berger, laying down the stencils and preparing to paint a traffic warning, hopefully right side up. Joe Jacoby stood next to Ralph. Joe's pickup was parked at the curb.

Nick couldn't resist the setup. As he approached the cones, he accelerated and angled a little to the left. The front bumper caught the first cone and sent it tumbling. Then the next cone, and the next. Thirty cones in all went flying. Ralph and Joe stood in shock and horror as they witnessed the devastation. Nick flew past them and continued down Springs Road. He looked in the rearview mirror and saw the two men climb into Joe's pickup, determined to chase down the perpetrator. Nick slowed, pulled over to the right, and stopped.

The pickup came to a screeching halt. Ralph and Joe jumped out of the truck and charged forward, ready to read the riot act, if not do bodily harm, to the driver of the old Chevy sedan. Nick rolled down the window and grinned. The two men stared at him and sputtered for a moment, their mouths wide open.

"Boots, goddamn it! Joe College, you SOB!" Then they doubled over with laughter.

Nick had executed the perfect prank. Thirty traffic cones—a new City of Vallejo record.

26

ome September, Nick had found his place and his rhythm in Charlottesville. Fall semester was underway and he was enjoying his classes. He'd moved into the Baseball House to that tiny cell in the basement. It had one major advantage: the rent was dirt cheap. He'd landed a part-time job tending bar at O'Neil's and the tips were good. Added to the money he'd saved from his city job, he was able to make ends meet. Fall baseball practice was also going well, and he believed there was a chance to earn a starting outfield position when spring rolled around.

Yes, he was a long way from home, but he was too busy to be homesick.

It was 3:00 p.m. and practice had been underway for about an hour on a hot and humid day—ninety degrees and ninety percent, a brutal combination. The field was set up for batting practice: a protective tarp spread over the infield, a beat-up batting cage rolled out to home plate, an L-screen set up to protect the batting practice pitcher. One hitter took his cuts while a handful, including Nick, waited to jump in for their swings. Coach Chip Murphy stood to the side of the batting cage, hitting ground balls to the infielders between pitches. Pitchers and catchers were gathered in the bullpen, getting in some work under the watchful eye of Head Coach Jim West. The rest of the squad was arrayed across the outfield, shagging batted balls and relaying them back to the infield.

The coach on the mound pitching batting practice was an intense young man from Louisiana, a new addition to the staff. His name was Antoine Thibodaux, and though he preferred to be called Tony, the players immediately dubbed him the Ragin' Cajun; RC for short.

Sweat poured from RC's body as he labored in the heat, doing his best to throw strikes for the hitters to rip. Around the outfield, players stood in small groups, talking and laughing. Some lounged against the fence, no one interested in hustling after batted balls.

They were lollygagging. RC could not tolerate lollygaggers.

He gave a shrill whistle and called everyone in, adding in the strongest terms that they'd damn well better run or there'd be hell to pay. The players double-timed it to the infield and gathered around the pitcher's mound. RC lit into them with all the fury he could muster.

"Damn it, y'all! You're loafin' out there! All y'all! Draggin' around the outfield, takin' it easy, half-assin' the balls back to the infield. God damn it, I ain't gonna stand for it. Remember, you practice the way you play, and you play the way you practice. I mean, look at me! I'm dyin' out here. My arm's hangin'. But I'm workin'. I'm gettin' the job done. I may be suckin' gas, but I'm getting it done. Hell, I'd suck anything—"

With that, a player standing behind RC broke up laughing. The coach spun around to confront the offender.

"Okay, damn it, what's so damn funny?"

"Oh, sorry, sir. I'm sorry. Nothing's funny, sir." The young man could barely maintain composure.

"Now, look. We are gonna stand here in the sun all day until you tell me what's so damn funny." RC was livid.

Seeing no way out, the player caved. "Well, sir … you said you'd suck anything."

Now four guys on the other side of the circle burst into laughter. The rest did their best to suppress snickers. To his credit, RC knew when he was licked. He couldn't let himself laugh, but he couldn't stifle a smile either. He directed one of the catchers to replace him on the mound to finish batting practice and sent everyone else back to their stations with an admonition to at least show some effort.

Nick soaked it all in and he loved it. These were his kind of guys. Three thousand miles from Vallejo, he was at home.

27

It was another warm September day, the sun dodging in and out behind puffy white clouds. Nick relaxed on the steps in front of the Rotunda, the iconic building designed by Thomas Jefferson. Just above him, on a granite pedestal, stood the statue of Jefferson, gazing off into the distance. Nick was a few minutes early to meet his date. He'd showered quickly after a fall practice session, collected his mail, and hurried the few blocks to the campus.

He watched, fascinated, as a crew worked to repair University Avenue using a paving machine, a massive Barber-Greene 395. He'd never seen one in action. It was an amazing process to watch. A dump truck, the bed raised to forty-five degrees, poured asphalt into a hopper at the front of the machine. A conveyor belt moved the material to a large rotating screw where it was spread and leveled. The rear section of the machine smoothed and tamped the asphalt firmly in place as it crept along at a steady pace, eight to ten feet per minute. The result: a perfect strip of pavement one lane wide. No crew with shovels. No magician named Don with a long-handled rake. No guy named Norm driving a metal-wheeled roller. Just a man in the truck, one controlling the Barber-Greene, and a couple of guys to clean up the excess that collected at the edges.

One guy holding a shovel out on University looked to be about Nick's age, maybe a little older. Nick wondered if Charlottesville was the young man's hometown and if he would agree that working on the street provided a whole new perspective. He thought about the streets of Vallejo that he knew so well. Sandy Beach Road, where the pavement ended and the boardwalk wound its way out to the Lighthouse. Lemon Street and the pier where he'd spent so many hours fishing with his buddies. The Lower Georgia district, with its dangerous reputation, former home to so many institutions—Parmisano and Sons Fish Market, the Farragut Club, the YMCA, the Carnegie Library. Along Marin Street, he pictured old city hall, the post office, and farther north, City Park and the Veterans Memorial Building where the all-night party was held after graduation. And Tennessee Street, home to Napoli Pizza, the El Rey Theater, Miracle Bowl, Patches Drive-In, and Scotty's Doughnuts. Then Nebraska Street and the Vallejo High campus, the eclectic mix of buildings looking more like a small college than a high school. And over on Broadway, Pluto's Hot Dogs—not Ralphie's Chicago-style, but damn good nonetheless. Finally, the old neighborhood—Steffan Manor—and the streets and homes and families he knew and loved, the best place on God's green earth to grow up. Nick looked at the young man out on University Avenue and wondered how well he knew the streets of Charlottesville. It would be a hoot to compare notes.

The bed of the dump truck banged down, jarring Nick from his reverie. He watched the empty truck pull away, a fully loaded one move in to take its place. He turned his attention to the two letters in his hand. One was from his mom and he opened it first. It was a long, newsy message. The closing lines read, "I'm sending the enclosed article from the *Times-Herald*. I thought you'd want to know." The clipping was from the society page of the Vallejo newspaper.

Engagements
Mr. and Mrs. Branford Foxworth announce the engagement of their daughter, Donna, to Dr. Elliot J. Margolis of Seattle, Washington.

The article provided a few more details, but Nick didn't read to the end. The second letter was from Gus Cordeiro, short and to the point.

Nick,
Mike Bouchka passed away on Labor Day. He died in his sleep. They say it was a heart attack.

Nick let the letters drop from his hands. Tears obscured his vision and he didn't see Kellen when she came up the steps to stand in front of him.

"Hi, Nick. Hey, what's up? Why so glum, chum?" Kellen attempted a smile.

"Hi, Kel. Sorry. Just some sad news from home."

Kellen took his face in her hands and kissed each eye in turn, taking away the tears. "Sorry, babe. Want to talk about it?"

"Sure. Let's get something to eat. Okay?"

"Okay. Anyplace but O'Neil's. Working there is bad enough without eating there all the time."

Nick laughed. He stood and took Kellen's hand as they descended the steps to street level. "Did I ever tell you about a guy named Mike Bouchka?"

"No. Is he a friend of yours?"

"Yeah, he was. Come on. I'll tell you all about him."

STREET CRED

They walked away down University Avenue, hand in hand.

Thomas Jefferson never blinked, staring unfazed into the distance. Perhaps he was thinking, *Where in the hell are Lewis and Clark? They damn well ought to be back by now.* Or maybe it was, *I wonder what good ol' Sally Hemmings is doing tonight? Maybe I'll stroll down to the slave quarters.* Whatever his thoughts, old Tom kept them to himself.

AUTHOR'S NOTE

Mark Twain's famous warning that opens *The Adventures of Huckleberry Finn* applies equally to *Street Cred*.

Notice

Persons attempting to find a motive in this narrative will be prosecuted;
persons attempting to find a moral in it will be banished;
persons attempting to find a plot in it will be shot.

If you were looking for motive, moral, and plot, it is likely you were disappointed. *Street Cred* is simply a story of a place and time and a peculiar group of characters. You could say it is in the spirit of *Cannery Row*. Let's acknowledge the obvious: Vallejo isn't Monterey, Lower Georgia Street isn't Cannery Row, and the author's name isn't Steinbeck. But, if you read the story just for fun, hopefully it made you smile.

Was 1970 a tipping point for the City of Vallejo? One could certainly make that case. The notorious Lower Georgia district was gone, flattened, ready for redevelopment, yet most Vallejoans would agree the promise of redevelopment was never matched by the execution.

In May 1970, when the USS *Drum* slid down the shipway, the nuclear submarine program at Mare Island Naval Shipyard came to an end. No one wanted to believe it at the time, but the shipyard's days were numbered. During World War II, civilian employment topped 46,000, and through 1970 it hovered around 12,000. That's a lot of jobs for a town the 1970 census counted at 71,710. By April 1996, that employment base was gone.

What happens to a shipyard town when it loses its shipyard? Most of what came next was not pretty. In June 2004, the Vallejo City Unified School District went into receivership administered by the State of California, requiring a $60 million emergency loan to continue serving students. It would not regain local control until April 2013.

In May 2008, Vallejo became the largest municipality in California to declare bankruptcy, finally emerging in November 2011. It became a case for other cities in financial meltdown to study.

There was another event, largely symbolic but impossible to ignore. In 1977, the stately and iconic Main Building at Vallejo High School was torn down, having been found deficient in earthquake standards. It was a building that stood for pride, tradition, and permanence, and though it was hard to watch the wrecking ball slam again and again into that beautiful structure, witnesses would say the old girl was a hell of lot tougher than she was given credit for.

Vallejo High has had its struggles since then. Some would say the troubles could be traced to rampant malfeasance in administration. One example: for more than a century, the Vallejo High symbol was the Apache, a tribute to a proud and valiant people. Without public input or consultation with Native American organizations, the school board voted one night to drop the Apache symbol. When alumni rose up in righteous anger and packed board meetings to ask for reconsideration, they were laughed at, hushed, and ignored. Now every April, old graduates flock to the campus for Alumni Day wearing T-shirts that proclaim, "Apaches Forever," because some traditions are hard to kill.

In spite of these troubles, many fine and successful families remain in Vallejo, building lives and raising children, generation after generation. They are joined in spirit by former Vallejoans everywhere, who continue to stand up for the community they love because they remember when it was "the best place at the best possible time."

ACKNOWLEDGMENTS

Diana Hwang began work on the cover while *Street Cred* was just an idea and then stayed with it through many iterations. Kim Rodda shared his expertise in the paving business, responding to my list of questions with careful attention to detail. Rob DeLiema and David Zweifel read the book as it was serialized on my blog and provided insightful comment and critique with each posting. Ruth Carter took what I thought was the finished product, flushed out my typical mistakes, and provided solid suggestions. Matt Spooner, Tom Campbell, Elizabeth Torphy, and Diana Pardee worked with me to craft the back cover copy.

To all the loyal, supportive, critical, caring people listed above, I offer a heartfelt thank-you.

Printed in the United States
By Bookmasters